P R

An Earthquake is a Shaking of the
Surface of the Earth

"Moschovakis's hallucinatory writing constellates the mind's obsessive recursions with precision. *An Earthquake Is a Shaking of the Surface of the Earth* undoubtedly raises the curtain to reveal her not-so-quietly standing among geniuses like Annie Ernaux, Joy Williams, and Clarice Lispector." —CLAIRE DONATO, author of *Kind Mirrors, Ugly Ghosts*

"Like Anna Kavan and Mary Shelley before her, Anna Moschovakis knows that the phone call is always coming from inside the building. *An Earthquake Is a Shaking of the Surface of the Earth* is a haunting in nine acts—a terrifyingly apt commentary on contemporary psychology, in which what has been lost is somehow too close to touch." —LUCY IVES, author of *Life Is Everywhere*

ALSO BY ANNA MOSCHOVAKIS

Participation: A Novel
Eleanor, or The Rejection of the Progress of Love
They and We Will Get into Trouble for This
You and Three Others Are Approaching a Lake
I Have Not Been Able to Get Through to Everyone

AN EARTHQUAKE IS A
SHAKING OF THE
SURFACE OF THE EARTH

A NOVEL

Anna Moschovakis

Soft Skull   New York

Copyright © 2024 by Anna Moschovakis

First Soft Skull edition: 2024

Library of Congress Cataloging-in-Publication Data
Names: Moschovakis, Anna, author.
Title: An earthquake is a shaking of the surface of the earth : a novel / Anna Moschovakis.
Description: First Soft Skull edition. | New York : Soft Skull, 2024.
Identifiers: LCCN 2024039445 | ISBN 9781593767839 (trade paperback) | ISBN 9781593767792 (ebook)
Subjects: LCGFT: Novels.
Classification: LCC PS3613.O7787 E27 2024 | DDC 813/.6—dc23/ eng/20240826
LC record available at https://lccn.loc.gov/2024039445

Cover design by Gregg Kulick
Cover art photograph © Deborah Stratman /
film still from For the Time Being *(2021)*
Book design by tracy danes

The title page is set in Lineal by Frank Adebiaye, with the contribution of Anton Moglia, Ariel Martín Pérez. Distributed by velvetyne.fr.

Soft Skull Press
New York, NY
www.softskull.com

Printed in the United States of America
10 9 8 7 6 5 4 3 2 1

For Maro

Why has no one erased the erroneous text?
Because one cannot erase letters of bronze?

HEDWIG DOHM, *Become Who You Are*,
translated by Elizabeth G. Ametsbichler

AN   EARTHQUAKE   IS   A

SHAKING   OF   THE

SURFACE   OF   THE   EARTH

I.

THEY SAY THAT walking is controlled falling, they say put one foot in front of the other, they say things will return to normal and you will adjust to the change, as if those are similar promises, and possible. They give you special equipment if you are deemed worthy of it, and if not, they assure you that you have special talents for adaptation. They call you *resilient*. If I am repeating what they say rather than what I think of what they say, it's because—not being resilient—I struggle with every step.

This morning, Tala showed me how she can cross

the room without even stumbling. I am ashamed to say she did this while carrying hot tea; her unoccupied arm was extended, undulating like the needle of some sensitive atmospheric dial. Elegant. "You only need one arm free to balance," she trilled, daring to turn her head around and smile at me as she closed in on the room's far wall. The smallest bit of amber tea sloshed from her cup then.

Tala is younger than me, by at least fifteen years (I can never recall her age: she is wise beyond it). Generally speaking, the younger are more resilient, of course.

She's gone out again, and I'm alone.

She goes out more and more now, leaving me to my teas and infusions, my stained carpet, my small view out the glass back door. Through it, from this scavenged daybed, I catch sight of the concrete square that was a patio, now fractured into jagged, unwalkable terrain. Squirrels darting around. The leftmost edge of the fruitless pawpaw tree. Our two bicycles, entangled and fallen, their tires flaccid, dusted with debris. The chain-link fence threaded with dull-green ivy, and above it: a sliver of sky, sliver of a downtown skyscraper sheathed in mirrors, reflecting more sky.

Do you ever really look at the sky, really look at it for long enough to let your mind wander away and then wander all the way back—back to the looking, and then further back to noticing what it is you're looking at, and how the sky is not a thing to be looked at, how the sky is not even a thing at all?

I want what Tala has. I'm not embarrassed to say it. I want her bony ankles and her wedge-heeled boots. I want the skin of her smooth forehead—*dewy*, there's no other word—and I want her dates and her friends. I want that high-pitched laugh that peals, even when there isn't much to laugh about. I don't care that it sounds fake sometimes, I don't care if it's a mask or a manipulation, if she's *crying inside*. It makes anyone who hears it happy: I want that.

("Do you want her, or do you want to be her?" a person I once knew wrote in a book, quoting their therapist. It has never occurred to me to ask if I want Tala *in that way*. She wouldn't have me, for one, and I don't like rejection. Sometimes I wonder if she's ever really looked at me at all.)

Wonder implies curiosity, implies delight. But it's also code for doubt—for unprocessed, perilous doubt, from which its whimsy can protect.

I protect myself, by which I mean I defend myself. And I have known for some time that the only way to get what I want from Tala is to kill her.

I CONSULT MY list. I try to keep it brief; I keep having to rewrite it to make sure the priorities *make sense*, that the priorities on the list match the priorities in my head. I don't like the feeling I get when they don't. What's it called? *Cognitive dissonance.* I never know what that means, really. You learn to mimic the language that gets you through the door. *Gets you through the door* is another example. Who taught that junk metaphor to me?

Door to what.

The list is in the kitchenette, on a strip of wall I painted with matte black paint so I can write on it with chalk. Faded white numbers, one through seven, line the left edge of the tall black rectangle; when I erase the list to rewrite it, I leave the numbers there. Out of laziness. Out of superstition. Lucky seven.

The list's daily revisions, if I had recorded them somehow, would make a good diary. An archive, open to interpretation.

Today's entry:

1. Coffee
2. Exercises—upper arms, back

3. Notebooks
4. Soak beans—flageolet (add kombu)
5. Balance
6. Calls—Insurance, C.
7. Lay groundwork

I can't, of course, put "Murder Tala" on the list. She would see it: it's right there in the kitchen we share, every morning and most nights, if I wait up for her. We sit around the red Formica table and watch wax drip from the candles I can't help but light at sundown, a little ritual for timekeeping, a stand-in for ritual. The thick drips pool into white amoebas on the red surface; sometimes we read them together, our futures or our pasts. At some point we'll run out of candles, I know.

"It's a speech bubble," Tala decided one night not long ago, frowning at a wax amoeba. "In your future. It means you haven't yet learned to say what you really mean." When she frowned, two small curves appeared above the corners of her mouth. Parentheses, in a delicate sans-serif font. Tala knows me, uncannily. It's true, I'm not ready to be rid of her just yet.

What I don't put on the list is what I spend most of my time actually doing. If thinking can be said to be doing, if planning can.

What would be the inverse of planning to kill Tala? Planning to let her live?

The more I stall—the more I leave off of the list— the more I wonder if I'm still moving properly in the direction of the future.

I once read a book whose protagonist's life project was to dig a hole. Then I had a dog whose life project was to dig a hole: the coincidence made me better understand the book. The dog is dead now and I gave the book away, but it left a *lasting impression*, as they say. (What kind of impression does not last?)

What I mean is that reading and witnessing are not the same thing. Let alone doing.

What I spend most of my life doing is, in a word, regretting. I was once like Tala. I crawled out from wherever they placed me ("they," *for lack of a better*)—I crawled out, hoping that something or someone would let me touch them, breathe on them.

I crawled out hoping, which it turns out looks a lot like dancing.

You should have seen me.

Tala goes dancing most nights, and I have asked her how they manage on the dance floor now, with all the aftershocks or whatever these movements are, these movements that convulse the ground beneath us, that almost never stop, not completely, so that now motion, rather than stillness, has become the rule. Stillness the exception *that proves it.*

Is it possible to imagine someone dancing in a way you can't, yourself, dance? When I imagine Tala dancing, I imagine her moving the way I once did, in slow, precise response to the music, secret-smiled and low-lidded, a sway that begins with an invisible inner impulse and pulses out from there, always in relation to another body or bodies—I mean to specific, countable bodies, whether acknowledged or not. Sometimes I would move so slightly, you might not call it moving at all. No, I don't imagine Tala dancing in the myriad unappealing ways I've seen others her age, at cast parties and in films, or on occasion at a club, dance—the hopping up and down as part of a throng, or the memorized friend-group choreographed bits, or the hypersexed flaunts à deux. I picture her familiarly, phenomenologically: a picturing from within. But I have no idea how Tala dances, how could I?

When I ask her *how they manage* she doesn't answer—doesn't even acknowledge the question. She just lets out that peal of laughter, throws back that lovely head.

THE LAST TIME I was cast in a play, it ended in disaster (of the *career-ending, unmitigated* kind).

I was perfectly up to the task: something ancient, an outdoor theater, actually two theaters a hundred feet apart, on a vast sloping lawn the audience was expected to traverse at will, choosing their adventure, each to each, depending on which aspect of the story most compelled them. The setting for this decentralized performance was a state park in the middle of the city. One of those parks that rise up improbably from neighborhoods and that, once you cross some trafficky boulevard and enter them, are designed to feel wild. In this case they'd succeeded, to a fault. Foraging happened there, and the rumored hunting of rabbits and birds. Mountain lion sightings were rare and attacks rarer, but not unheard of. Once, a crocodile showed up in the duck pond at the park's edge and had to be shot by some city entity nobody had ever heard of called Wildlife Evict & Rescue.

The park and the theater aren't more than a couple of miles from this bungalow, this bed. They feel so far.

The disaster occurred in the third act, in the final performance of the play's final run, in a scene that involved a ritual slaughter in which I was the one with the knife.

The speech I was delivering was hectic, opaque. I'd had to call upon all of my training to fill the outdated words with life. It was the Sunday matinee: the sun had begun to dip in the sky—we were well past the solstice, though that wouldn't have struck me then—and was positioned, not accidentally on the part of the production designers, to serve as a spotlight for this scene. A spotlight for me, for my speech. My lower lip trembled as I raised the knife and shrieked.

There is something that happens when the audience is with you. Just because attempts to describe it are always pathetic—always self-serving, canned, tied to metaphors that not only fail as metaphor but that fail on their own terms (as if an actor wants the audience *frozen, hypnotized,* or *wrapped around their finger,* wants it *eating from the palm of their hand*)—doesn't make it untrue. There is something that happens when the audience is with you.

And there is something that happens when it turns on you.

My memory of that moment is unclear. In my memory, people suddenly rose from the crowd, in several small clusters. Signs, screams, banners, red paint, eggs. A protest, against something—my speech? My character's imminent, violent act? I stood there, knife high. I went up on my lines, first time in years.

One cohort of the protesters was chanting something I couldn't understand, quietly, beneath their breath. They were the charismatic ones—they threw nothing, they didn't scream, it wasn't clear whose attention they were trying to get—and they were the ones who caused me (or perhaps only invited me) to halt the performance and address the audience with an apology that rose up in me from who-knows-where.

I don't recall how the apology began. It wasn't much, I wasn't eloquent. The sun was fully in my face. Against that brightness, everything went dark. The strangest sensation occurred in me then. I have tried to find words for it ever since. Tried and failed. The best I can do is to say that, for an instant, all separation between myself and others vanished. Not a melting or a fusing, more a disintegration or a dissolution. But none of those descriptions are right.

When I say "others" I don't mean only other people—the audience, the yelling protesters, the murmuring witches, the stagehands in the wings—but also other things, both tangible and not: I mean the stage itself, the stage sets, the portable footlights and movable backdrops; I mean the birds and the sounds they were making, the grass and the boulders beyond, the trees; I mean the clothes I was wearing and the clothes everyone was wearing. I mean even the prop knife in my own hand. This is what I remember.

"I need you to know that it's breaking," I said. I was miked; my soft words traveled electronically through the air.

"Something is happening," I said. "Something is happening that I don't understand. I'm only telling you so that whatever happens next, you'll know why."

The sensation passed, and I could see what was in front of me again. By which I mean that I could feel there was again a *me* in front of which the *what* remained.

I should say that, now, the audience was with me again. Not in the way they were with me before the interruption. In the other way, the better way, for which there is no battery of bogus metaphors. The way we actors don't even bother trying to describe.

I directed the rest of my address to the charismatic ones. Downstage left. I was neither brilliant nor original, but I remember the feeling of believing what I said.

"You're right, you're right—We don't know what we're doing—We don't know what we're doing and we keep doing it anyway—We keep doing it anyway—But I should speak for myself—I should only speak for myself—But I'm an actor—I don't speak, I repeat— Just an actor—Interprète—I only repeat—Rehearse—

Repeat—Rehearse—Repeat—How strange . . . How
strange . . . I never noticed—I somehow never noticed
how there's a *hearse* in *re*—"

And then the knife dropped from my hand, and I
fell to the stage and vomited.

"You were wonderful," said the assistant stage manager
as I puked into the patch of grass where he had stationed
me, or us: he sat close, knees hugged to his chest, trying
mostly to avoid looking at me, as if wanting to offer some
privacy to my misery. "I'm ashamed to say that before this
production I'd never seen you in anything. Your face is so
familiar, though, especially seeing you now, so close up."

An afternoon chill had fallen. Everyone but the assistant stage manager and I had disappeared. Beyond the
low temporary fence that outlined the theater grounds,
people walked dogs, buttoned sweaters and zipped up
jackets. I kept vomiting, and the world kept happening
around me, separate from me, though more tenuously
so. The world happened, and I stayed separate from it,
barely, by which I mean that despite myself I kept trying
to *take it in*.

An aster is a member of the planet's second-largest family of plants, to which many people are allergic. Its flow-
ers resemble stars. A *disaster* is a conflict or a dissonance,

a problem between what people want and what the stars want for them. In any game, one player's disaster can be another's win.

Eventually, I stopped vomiting. The assistant stage manager had clearly been instructed not to leave my side, but also clearly wanted to go to the cast party, which would have been well underway. I convinced him that I had someone waiting for me at home. I convinced him that it would be enough to drop me off at the entrance to the park, that it was barely ten blocks between there and where I lived, and I would relish the walk.

It's interesting to try to recall this now. The feeling of exaggerated relief was one thing—I forgot to mention how, throughout my time with the assistant stage manager, I was repeating the one sentence it seemed possible to say: "I want to die"—how it becomes clear, at the end of every episode of extreme panic, pain, or fear, that the opposite of *intolerable* isn't *tolerable* but something more like *ecstatic*. But there was another, less esoteric sensation, with everything grown brighter and more sharply defined than usual, as if the separation between me and others, between me and not-me, was now reasserting itself with an exaggerated insistence. A chain-link fence overlooking a vast undeveloped lot lined the first part of my path home, which went along a concrete overpass; chiaroscuro clouds and peeling billboards floated above the sunken pit, which evened out as I walked its length and became a parking lot for a fleet of yellow school buses. I walked and stopped to look, walked some more. It was hard to believe I'd been so abject an hour before.

Of course, the ecstatic feeling didn't last. Soon after I reached the end of the overpass, I turned into the first alley I saw and sank down to my heels beside a dumpster.

The sunset had finally arrived, intensified by smog, a blooming purple bruise. I was paralyzed with exhaustion. I tried to make sense of the graffiti on the side of the dumpster. I watched the color leave the sky. I became aware of the sound of running water nearby, with no discernible source, and when I was able to stand again and walk a few steps, I saw that the sound came from a small fountain mounted to a pole attached to a sign that read MOTEL, and below it in white marquee letters, SHO TIME.

First I drank from the fountain—how dehydrated I must have been!—and then I walked up to the door and went inside. My bungalow felt miles away, and I could muster only steps.

THE MORNING PAPERS were dribbled with venom. I picked one up in the lobby as I checked out from the motel, after a dull, heavy sleep between coarse pink sheets.

In the papers, the consensus was *unfortunate*. The consensus was *drugs*. They taunted me from the news-stands as I walked home, past a stretch of storefronts that had been in flux for years, with small businesses opening and failing sequentially, a palimpsest of color schemes and partly legible signs.

A television in the window of what might have been a gallery or might have been somebody's apartment— there was no sign, no mailbox, no vinyl letters on the plate glass—slowed my steps. White letters on a black screen flashing one phrase at a time.

FOR THE TIME BEING
IN THE INTERIM
IN THE COURSE OF TIME
FROM DAY TO DAY

I didn't stop to wait for what would come next, though I continued the list in my head as I walked past.

IN THE MOMENT

IN DUE TIME
WHEN THE TIME IS RIGHT
SUDDENLY
EVERLASTING
NOW

LATER, I FOUND out the charismatic protesters were witches. Tala told me: one of them was her friend (her friends were numerous, unfathomable—at that point, I longed to be one of them). The witches had been upset not because of the performed slaughter of a stuffed goat but because they had taken it upon themselves to protest misinformation about ritual, to resist the surface co-optation of ritual by commercialization, capitalism, white supremacy, by (for example) publicly funded performances sanctioned by the state. They had been happy (or at least Tala's friend reported that they had been happy) with my awkward but earnest apology, and this rescued something for me. It helped me to feel that the loss of a job, and the probable loss of a career, was not without meaning.

And there was loss. I was a working stage actor, not a household name. The company that mounted the plays in the park was a large city-affiliated nonprofit and a regular employer of mine. It provided a significant percentage of my income, next to the waning residuals from a handful of national commercials that in their own way had probably lowered my *cultural capital* (and might explain my fuzzy familiarity to the assistant stage manager).

In the weeks after I'd alienated the establishment with my apology—my betrayal—I was approached by members of the experimental underground who remembered me from a cult play I'd been in long ago, and who now offered me parts in low-budget productions that rehearsed during the day, since most actors in that scene worked their money jobs at night. My money job, as a long-term temp—a stable but irregular gig I took on when the commercials stopped airing and I failed to land new ones—was in an office. Now, it was all I had. This was the excuse I gave, at least. Mostly to myself. Did I also think I was too old to work in underground theater for scale, or less? Either on principle, or as a biological, endurance-related fact? Whatever the reason or reasons, I said no to the young directors, and then no again, and then I stopped being asked. How quickly they stopped asking.

Tala moved in that month, taking over half of my tiny bungalow and a quarter of its mortgage. There was some talk of my giving her voice lessons too, for a few extra dollars a week, but that never materialized. I would have liked it. But I was too intimidated to remind her, and after that initial conversation she never brought it up again.

The movements, the shaking, the cracking of the concrete patio, began shortly after she moved in.

Soon after that, I stopped paying the mortgage altogether. As far as I know, everybody did.

I MUSTN'T LET my muscles atrophy. Each day I practice balancing. Standing on both legs, standing on one leg (while gripping something, usually the counter of the kitchenette, with both hands). Heel lifts, toe lifts. Walking, when I can. I'll take a series of the smallest, safest steps, holding on to whatever is in reach: the counter, the back of a chair, the bookshelf. Sometimes I stand without support and try to remember what it felt like to do a full set of pliés with ease. Sometimes, instead, I conjure the lesson I learned from a sailor on a boat off the coast of Brittany (I must have been the age Tala is now)—balance as a full-body practice that begins and ends with the gut.

The sailor and I had no language in common, so he taught with his hands: he touched me, and I moved.

Face this way. Pull this up and this in. Here, here, here.

The primary muscle group I am exercising, though, is not located in my legs, or in my *core* (the sailor's missing word). The day I halted my own performance, after the disorientation on stage and the vomiting off of it, after I had checked into the cheap motel and placed my unfamiliar body on the unfamiliar bed, the sensations that had accumulated began to add up into the first new feeling I could remember having in years. I still have no words for it, or too many of them. A blurriness at my edges that was also a shimmer. A lightness that was also a ground. Like the opposite of vertigo. As if I were, all at once but not instantly, both less and more myself. (And other inadequate sentences too numerous to copy out here.)

Everything that has happened since then began with that feeling. The muscles I'm working to train were born on that day.

> *edge to edge, never over the edge*
> *tell it to me taut / bandage / sore*
> *I might have something better soon*
> *there are fixtures / they break*
> *revolver, revolve*
> *if gather won't gather*
> *find one—*

II.

WHAT MAKES A person go off the deep end? (Another junk metaphor, inherited from whom? Just try to draw a picture of it—you can't. And yet, we think we know what it means.)

J.P. showed up an hour ago. He knocked four times, struck me out of my thinking exercises, out of my project. The visit was unexpected. He is one of those people. He comes and goes, who knows where; his bungalow, just steps away from mine, has been dark for months. Even when he's around, he's only passing through.

The last time I saw him, we sat together on the

concrete patio that was still a patio—flat and solid, imagine!—and sipped iced tea made from garden mint and sage. There is barely room for the two chairs, the little table between them, the margin of weeds, the bikes. Beneath the table, it's possible for two people's knees to touch. J.P. had seemed changed that day, I remember. Sturdier. Almost no time had passed since my disaster, the vomiting, the motel. The papers. (Rumors, he'd told me, were starting to *spread*.)

Was it just the next day? That afternoon even, after I'd walked home at last, leaving behind the gallery or apartment window with its strange video, with its awkward phrases about time? There had been an image on the monitor too, cycling with the words—*looping*—of a vast crater and a small blue sky, a crater big enough to swallow the world. I remember the feeling of aftermath. I remember the taste of apology and abandon in my mouth.

Over tea, when I noticed him changed—sturdier—I remember wondering if it was J.P. who'd changed or if it was me.

Today is different. Today, I don't know what to think. He showed up, yelled his name by way of identification. "You're going to want to hear what I have to say!" he called out at a lower volume.

I used the small plastic remote Tala had brought home for me—stolen, probably, but it was a nice gesture that I accepted with a smile. I had to click it twice, but then the door swung open, and there was J.P. in all of his—what do they say?—*splendor.*

He staggered over to me, the whole six-foot-plus of him, his pale skin chapped, his hair stringy and thinning and longer than ever, his five-o'clock shadow newly white, as if he'd aged on an accelerated timeline since that last visit.

"Look what I found," he said first, and pulled from his jacket pocket a single, perfect artichoke. "For you. And your friend."

He looked around, presumably for Tala, and saw she wasn't home—the door to her room was open, and there is no place else to hide. I answered his glance with a shake of my head. "Good," he said, and lurched into the chair across from me just as a strong and prolonged tremor shook the room.

Shimmer, glimmer.

What happened next was what always happens with J.P., but more, and worse. In the beginning, he bends your ear with something incontrovertible, with a theory of the present that builds on premises you share: something suspicious about the endless tremors, probably fracking-related, multinational conglomerate–related;

something suspicious about the well-stocked grocery stores (monopoly-related, Big Ag); something especially suspicious about the de facto loan forgiveness, the disappearance of some, but not all, utility bills; the rent freeze, the mortgage freeze, the general uneasy—if (or because) welcome—lightening of everyone's load. The theory then expands into its own periphery, way out, dissipating and settling at the same time, the way smoke becomes stench.

I'm used to these rants. To the commingling of the incontrovertible with the unfounded, to the charade of inevitability of J.P.'s pseudo-logical act. He has charm, so his speeches have charm: that wayward intelligence shining from his green-brown eyes, it can be hard to leave their glow.

Before the ground physically started to shake, I would describe conversations with J.P. in this way: how first you're just talking, first you're delighted or bemused, and it goes on, and it goes on and it goes on. And then, the ground you're standing on starts to move. A stutter. Something with the beat, a loss. And now? Now that there's no beat, only loss?

"It's going to stop, and you're going to realize that it never really happened" is what he kept repeating this time, with an urgency and redundancy that felt new, unyielding. It went on that way; he took advantage of each pause in the tremors to walk calmly around the room, his long arms outstretched. "See? Look, Ma, no hands!" It was fine, it was entertaining even, or if not exactly entertaining, then it was information, until finally it—or I—became so confused, so shook, it was no longer anything.

How his long arm outstretched resembles Tala's long arm outstretched, undulating.

I asked J.P. to leave. He didn't want to. I asked again, he refused again. Finally, as if woken from his trance by the shaft of sunlight that arrives at some point on every sunny morning to transform this room, he turned to go, first shoving a slim, gloss-white brochure into my hand.

"Just . . . Just ask yourself about *her*," he said dramatically over his shoulder when he was already halfway out the door. "Listen to your instincts. What makes you think she's telling you the truth?"

His eyes were shining. The shine seemed to stay behind after he left.

It hung in the air, hovering with intent.

I DIDN'T OPEN the brochure. I held it, staring at its glossy front in a fog. The light made dark shapes on its bright surface, quicksilver abstractions, which prevented the words from capture. FL__R__LF it seemed to read, in big block type. Then, __N_OUR__SE__.

So, so tired. I must have slept on the daybed for hours. When I woke, the sun had moved around the side of the house again, and a breeze came through the window that had brought its light. I noticed then that the window was cracked: a small hole, the size of a lime, in the middle of the lower pane. No idea when, or how. I leaned over and brought my eye to the hole. A rabbit rustled in the strip of dirt by the chain-link fence. A rabbit? I blinked. A squirrel.

A ragged brown squirrel, looking down, doing something with its hands.

I felt behind me for J.P.'s brochure, which I'd left on the side table. There was nothing there.

TALA DIDN'T COME home. I shouldn't be surprised. I rose at my accustomed time and peered into the kitchenette, expecting to see her there, as usual, brewing coffee for us both in the midnight-blue robe she wore almost always around the house (she has two settings, Tala: *home* and *out*). I shouldn't be surprised. But I was shocked to find her gone. Something deeper than shock. Shattered, struck. Like the patio. Like the window. A hole.

That was where we'd sat across from each other, night after night. That was where we'd sometimes sat next to each other instead. Where we had studied spilled wax, and interviewed each other about our pasts, where we had *shared*.

Had we shared? Histories, pain, memories recounted. Like and unalike. Did we hand pieces of these things to each other? One for one, each to each? I'll cut the cake, you choose the slice you want.

There is a power in desire.

I have wanted Tala gone. I have dreamed of it, and planned it. I have made sense of my own unhappiness by reverse-twinning it to her happiness. Apparent happiness, that is—she remains a mystery to me—

I ate my millet with slices of apple. The ground was uncommonly still, almost stable, and through the compromised window that no longer divided indoors from out, I could tell it was a bright, warm day. Fence, sky, and distant skyscrapers formed a vexing collage in the window's frame. I decided, for the first time since the world had been as it was, to get dressed and venture out.

There was a chance, after all.

There is a power in desire.

OUTSIDE, AND THE skyscrapers look bigger and less real, separated from their frame. Outside and the day is calm, still, the street empty, layered with a fine, beige sand. Small banks of sand at its edges, like after a strong wind. But there is no wind.

Has it been still out here all this time? Has the ground only moved beneath my little house, my bungalow? A figure hustles by on the opposite side of the street, hood up. I consider speaking, but my mouth is as slow as my mind, and by the time I form the beginnings of a vowel, *ahhhhhh*, *uhhhhhh*, the figure's gone.

I've brought my cane, but I'm not using it. I drag it along beside me, my middle finger crooked around its handle, and draw a solitary track in the shallow sand. It's ugly, the cane. I hate it. But it draws a pretty track.

The question about whether it's been still out here is not my question. It's a question J.P. put in my head, along with everything else. I need to pay attention to these things. To stay awake.

When Tala moved in, a challenge arrived with her. It called to me.

Approaching her unexpected presence was like approaching a giant rock. A giant, sheer rock face, the kind that *looms*, with a rumored paradisiacal beach on the other side—a pot of gold awaiting the climber who doesn't give up. With my fear of heights, my fear of exposure, to scale it would be impossible. Or, if not impossible—if I found or faked the nerve to make it over the ridge—I'd be so slow, I'd take so long, the beach would be dark by the time I arrived. The climb an embarrassment, the beach trip a failure, I'd die of exhaustion or of cold.

When Tala moved in, I knew one of these failures was inevitable—failure to launch, or failure to land—just not which one. But the call was strong: long-lost stirrings for the experience of touching someone new, for the confusion of it, for the feeling of being thrown.

Who was in love with whom back then, when I was Tala's age, even before? I mean all of us, all at once—were we assigned lovers at random, or did it just feel that way? Or if by design, by whose?

Did the sheer rock face, impossible obstacle, appear from nowhere at some point (instantly, or slowly but without our notice) in the interval between then and now? Was I deluded then, or am I deluded now?

Whose questions are these. Whose gold pot.

I emerged dancing, I told you already. Now, I can barely get from there to here.

When Tala arrived, *from nowhere,* nothing looked the same. The possible had bled through its container, like the skyscrapers through their frame. Tala became the missing piece, the perspectival shift.

Tala, Tala. No metaphor too great. New leaf. Blank slate. Invention of the wheel.

THE VIEW BEFORE me opens up, without offering any further information. Vaster avenues, more fine sand, brighter sun, taller buildings. A different overpass, I think. No fountain, no motel. A multiplication of hooded figures scurrying by. I know this city. I'm *from* it. It's always been this way.

I too have been this way. Same script in my head, same loop.

I've long understood I'm not perfect. That the only answer to an imperfect life would be a perfect death. For much of my life, each year—twice, on the verge of spring and on the verge of fall—I would vow to die. And, each year, twice, on the first morning of spring and the first morning of fall, I would will myself to wait.

I could wish to wish to die, but I could not wish to die. Another failure. The evidence of this habit is ample, is *on the record* in black and white, sometimes in blue.

And then there was my disaster, and then there was the question in my mouth: *But what if the perfect death doesn't have to be mine?* And then, soon after, there was Tala.

I've seen enough. I feel the tremors starting back up, and now I'm using my cane, and soon any surface within reach: building walls, curbside trees, the sides of parked cars. Just to keep from toppling. It takes an eternity to get myself home.

"THEY'RE CALLED FAIRY lights," she said as she strung the copper wires above the tiny cement patio, threading them around the bungalow's gutter on one side and along the top of the chain-link fence on the other three.

Between patio and fence were the slim margins of dirt, tumbling with weeds—with weeds that are herbs, herbs that are weeds.

"They turn on automatically when the sun goes down," she'd said, a slight turn, slight smile.

Tonight, dusk fell bluntly soon after my return; the moon is full, or almost, its cool white glow dissonant with the dim amber warmth of the dotted strings.

It's awkward, this thing.

I look at my list.

5. Make tea
6. Find J.P.'s brochure

So, I'll do both.

MIDNIGHT, WOKEN BY a violent shake. Tala is still gone, day three of her absence. I should move into her bedroom. It's getting risky sleeping out here on the daybed, so narrow and exposed. Tala's bed is normal, full-sized, taking up the bulk of the vacant room. By the moon's light I rise and stagger to it, tuck myself into her deep-blue sheets, sleep.

In the morning, it's bright out the window. Green on blue, washed. A weak breeze lifts the edge of the bed-sheet. The glossy white brochure lies open in my hand.

WHAT DID YOU DO WHEN YOU
WERE MOST YOURSELF?

WHEN DID YOU STOP?

WHAT WOULD IT TAKE FOR YOU
TO DO IT AGAIN?

DO YOU BELIEVE IN PAST LIVES?

WHAT OR WHO IS HOLDING YOU
BACK?

ANNA MOSCHOVAKIS

HOW WOULD YOU FEEL IF THEY
WERE GONE?

Send your completed questionnaire to
Box 6532, Center City.

THE WEEK AFTER Tala moved in, taking over the single bedroom and displacing me to the living room, to the daybed (a displacement I intended, I admit, for her to *feel* without being overtly reproached for it), I knocked on her door with a cup of coffee and asked if she had time for a chat. It had occurred to me that I didn't know much about her, that what I did know about her felt as if I'd received it at the end of a game of telephone, partial and unreliable, like a decades-old memory.

I knew her to be social, to be confident. I knew she had been raised in a city—I think—or near enough to one. Near enough to disdain those who weren't. I knew her to be broadly *competent*, *impressive*: physically, mentally, interpersonally. I listed these traits to her as we sat sipping coffee side by side on her bed.

"And yet, you don't know me at all," Tala had responded. She was perched on the edge of the blanketed mattress, wearing those wedge-heel boots and some kind of loose, structured dress. Black over black. Her voice was quiet but powerful, in a way that suggested she was conserving its considerable volume for when she, or when the world, might need it. As if her voice was *not working up to its potential*.

"Because these words you're saying, these descriptions, are only things that people say about me, and what I really feel myself to be is something very different. In fact,"—she breathed deeply through her nose; her eyes narrowed, then relaxed—"you might as well negate each of the things you've just said, replace each claim with its opposite, and you'd get closer to having a picture of who I am."

She stopped suddenly then and stared into the room, not at me, not at anything.

"But you won't, will you? People always believe their own projections more than what they're told by the source. It's okay. Where we do agree is that this collection of traits you just recited is, in a way, a description of me. It's a lie, but it's the lie I'm forced to live."

She finished her coffee, peered in my direction with a small protective squint.

"Can I go?"

This scene never repeated itself in any version or variation; Tala evaded whatever approaches to intimate talk I made from then on. She was so open about certain things: the names of the friends she was going out to meet (and how eager she was to go out to meet them); how she fell into her line of work, which as far as I could tell was to raise money for other people and organizations in exchange for a cut of the eventual take. I would say "grant writer" but there seemed to be very little writing involved—she mostly *took* meetings, *connected* people, *advocated* for causes, and *followed up* on leads. In another era, she said, her calling would have been *matchmaker*.

There was something martyr-like in how Tala described her profession, tinged with self-erasure. "I'm like the ladder that gets shoved away when it's no longer of use."

When the tremors pause, I get up to strip Tala's bed but lose momentum before gathering my own sheets from the daybed and instead lie down on her bare mattress, her blue sheets loose and tangled on the floor. Absent to myself, staring again at the white brochure.

What or who is holding you back // How would you feel if they were gone?

> *forging a joint through what we know as arid*
>   *and slack*
> *figuring, as in to fathom*
> *signature depth, signature fake*
> *the one reads smoothly and the other dents*
> *mothers and fathers and friends are politic*
> *underscored by figured night*
> *is this the fact in the corner? is that the trash?*

III.

CELIA CALLS. I let it go to voicemail, knowing my mailbox is full. Then regret it: I wonder what she wants. She could be calling to report a sighting of Tala! In person, or in some old photograph that has happened to reappear, in a box, or on a screen. She is the one person who knew us each before we knew each other. With both of us, Celia *goes way back*. It must be strange for her.

We have spent only one evening together, the three of us, at Celia's husband's house (she always refers to it this way, as it makes her queasy to own such a comfortable home, one she couldn't have purchased *on her own*.)

The house is modern and sun-drenched, and the three of us had beers on the deck that overlooks Celia and her husband's hilly neighborhood of mostly one-story houses with gardens, interrupted by a low self-storage building painted orange and white, substrate for a shifting script of illegal signs, illegal murals, wheat-pasted posters, spray-painted graffiti. Where was the husband? No idea. This could not have been long ago, though it feels distant now.

After the beers we pulled down all the shades and watched a film Tala wanted to see, one that had come up in conversation, she said, with people whose opinions mattered, by which I felt she meant by people she wanted to impress. Tala set it up to stream on her laptop, since Celia claimed not to know how to hook up her husband's big flat-screen.

We sat in a row on the stuffed leather couch, sharing a bag of microwave popcorn, one or the other of us wincing periodically at a scene of animal torture or animal death. ("I guess they weren't unionized back then," Tala said, maybe joking, though her expression was tight.)

After it ended we drank more, and I listened as the two of them talked.

Tala gushed about the sets, the costumes, the colors. Celia seemed annoyed, said something about how the film was unfair to Christianity, how Christianity in the film was being willfully misconstrued, and how even though she was not Christian she was sensitive to these things. Tala looked at Celia like she was a hundred years old. For my part—for who else's part could I speak?—*for my part*, I felt something different, something violent and raw, outside aesthetics or ideas. I felt betrayed.

By which I mean, I felt seduced. Stricken with envy of these actors—beautiful, beautiful bodies! Bodies *of every shape and size*. Bodies swaying, climbing, spinning, pounding, striking, being struck; combining and separating, forming shapes and breaking shapes; obeying and disobeying one another, recognizing and un-recognizing one another; wearing nothing or wearing masks or wearing uniforms; becoming uniform, becoming crowd, un-individuated, un-separate, un-human. Becoming object, becoming matter. A feeling I knew, as an actor, and feared I might never experience again.

Or a feeling I only wanted, desperately, to have known, that I had chased with every arrival to rehearsal, with every first entrance on every opening night, every last bow. I had always struggled with self-consciousness: the image of my body in my head. Not the actors in this film. The feeling among them was only abundant, un-measured, contagious—I was sure of it. Something that can't be faked. How I would have liked to play in those orgiastic, ecstatic scenes! My skin rubbed down with oil, head shaved, throwing my limbs around for the camera, touching and being touched. Dancing.

I watched Celia and Tala talk, watched them argue and repair. But I was elsewhere, falling.

I had a good teacher once, who met with me to discuss a complicated video I'd made for an assignment and who, at the end of our conference, said, "You mean what you're trying to get at is just _____? And you want to make me work that hard to figure it out?"

No, not you, I thought but could not say. The work is hard. But it isn't yours to do.

I heard Celia say, "And then to end by announcing it's all an illusion?"

I heard Tala say, "And all those animals had to die for this?"

CELIA AND I were coworkers then, and still are, technically, though we're on indefinite furlough now. So I doubt this morning's phone call was about work, though it's true she remains more plugged-in than I do, generally, and might have some fresh *goss* (as Tala would say, daring me not to understand).

I don't want goss, not about work. The only thing I want from Celia now is Tala's present location.

I HAVE SUCCEEDED, at least, in moving back into Tala's room, now no longer her room.

I have consolidated her things into half of the closet, and half of the dresser drawers. A pile of hard-to-store things in the corner: yoga mat, weights, a guitar case missing its guitar.

I took down the curtain so I can be woken by the sun.

I know it may not seem it, but I am serious about getting rid of her. I am *gathering my forces*.

I may not be ready yet. I am not ready yet. But the question isn't whether, it's how. It's when.

I'll gather the force of the sun when it's in my face.

I HAVE BEEN haunted by yesterday's walk outdoors. By what I saw and by what I didn't see. So few people on the streets, they must be inside the buildings. But the buildings don't tell us what they know.

Actors develop a sixth sense, can detect when other bodies are near. It did not *feel* to me that those buildings contained people. The buildings in question are offices and houses, are apartments and mixed-use dwellings. Every kind of building. They did not feel full.

But there is another explanation for the haunting. I've always been an actor. But when I try to articulate this other explanation, when I say, "I don't know who I am if no one's looking at me," it isn't my profession I'm referring to. When I suggest that, on yesterday's walk, it wasn't the absence of others from my view that gave me the feeling of an emptied world, but the absence of myself from the view of others, I am suggesting a problem not with the world but with the self. A problem with, or of, my self.

How silly. How unnecessarily complex. Every project is contained by projection—it's right there in the word.

Scratch an actor, you'll find another actor. Laurence Olivier said that. Though someone else probably said it first.

I needed a witness, and Tala showed up. Now she's gone.

I HAVE TO go out again. No other option. If I don't, I'll disappear.

I respond to Celia's "Your mailbox is full" text with an invitation to meet me in an hour. "At the bar," I type, "whether or not it's still there."

But the tremors are too constant and too strong to risk it now. When I bend down to pick up my shoes, I fall over. Celia delays anyway, replies "tmrw nite better for me." And now the sun is dropping, the silence of evening.

I used to love evening. All those eyes on me, the flattering light.

WHAT DID YOU DO WHEN YOU
WERE MOST YOURSELF?
Conversations with strangers

WHEN DID YOU STOP?
Asphyxiated

WHAT WOULD IT TAKE FOR YOU
TO DO IT AGAIN?
Strangers, subjects, locale, mood, voice

I fell asleep with the brochure under my chin. Maybe I drooled on it, just a little. Enough for the words *stranglers* and *subtexts*, in bleeding blue ballpoint ink, to manifest, then greet me in the morning light.

I WENT TO the bar to meet Celia. A happy-hour date, which meant I left the house as the sun dropped low, and walked into it.

I trudged unaided down the sand-swept street, dragging my cane along my side. When I got to the overpass, I stopped to look through the fence at the trashed billboard, the yellow school bus fleet.

Did I see another person? A moving car? The dipping sun made it hard to see, hard to know. But I don't think it was solely responsible for my sense of being utterly alone.

Because I was looking, scanning, for signs of life, specifically for signs of street life. As I kept walking I kept expecting the familiar, scenes from the recent past. The rows of tents with their silent occupants; the patches of ground that passed for plazas or squares, with their gregarious ones.

I finally passed a few indistinct figures, like those I'd encountered the last time. Shuffling by, not looking at me. Not looking at me at all.

Unlooked-at, adrift, I called after one of them—"Is anything open?"—and received a suspicious glance in return. The figure's mouth moved, and then one of the figure's arms gestured three times in the same manner, and then the figure hurried off.

I made the gesture the figure had made. Like throwing a ball, but gently. A ball that didn't have far to go.

THE BAR WAS open, apparently, though everything happening inside seemed muted, fogged.

There were people—not crowded, not empty—a *scene*. I couldn't see their faces, it was dark, lit only by dozens of glass-bound candles. A red hue suffusing the place. Loud music, surround sound, a dusky vocal, old. It was warm, I took off my coat and looked around for Celia. Nobody noticed me. I found a stool at the bar with another empty one next to it.

The bartender looked like Tala: same dark long hair, same smooth skin. A sleeve of floral tattoos, blue-black nails. I ordered a whiskey and pulled out my book. My cane, which I'd propped against the bar, kept sliding down and clanging on the floor, so I had to stoop to pick it up. When it dropped for a third time, I left it there.

The book I was reading, or about to begin reading, was a book about Method acting. It had been on my pile for some time, inert, but now it felt necessary and called to me, as if it had arrived with an embedded timer set for this day.

The book interested me on principle because of my experience, my *track record*, with the Method. But more important now was that one of its authors (the book had two authors and was written as a kind of conversation) was a person Tala had mentioned knowing, and—as this was also a person I knew, or at least had once known, somewhat—the coincidence offered a point of connection between us, Tala and me. A connection that, in the wake of her disappearance, became a space for me to dwell.

I would have to dwell alone. These days, I can't talk to Celia about Tala, can't even mention her name. I'll get a blank stare, more than blank, silencing: that stare a person gives you when they've misheard what you've said and will not be asking for clarification. The more-than-blank stare is a look that willfully rejects, excludes, denies, *annuls*. I can't talk to Celia about Tala directly, so I came to the bar prepared with more oblique tactics. Picturing her approaching me with this book in my hand was one.

Before I'd read more than a page, Celia did approach, looking sour. She perched on the stool by my side, did something with her hair that changed the way she appeared, and ordered something to drink, a cocktail with a name I didn't recognize. The bartender's blue-black nails flashed and fluttered like little dancers as she pulled ingredients out of bins and bottles off shelves.

"You look like hell," Celia said. "I barely recognize you."

She reached up then and smoothed my hair over my scalp, like you'd pet a dog.

"Are you broke? Do you have food?"

Celia didn't seem to expect answers to these questions. She turned to accept her complicated drink from the bartender and sipped it, nodding her appreciation. Her face had an entirely different expression when it was directed toward the Tala look-alike with the deep-brown hair and the blue-black nails. When she turned back to me, the sourness—a tight, deflated quality, as if someone had let the air out of her face—returned. I immediately forgot about my oblique tactics, my imagined lighthearted chatter about the coauthor of the book I was holding, chatter I'd imagined—pulse quickening—leading naturally to a mention of Tala.

No. I could tell that this would be a conversation to endure, not to control.

Celia was using her furlough time to paint, she told me, after a silence that measured how long it took for her to be certain I would disappoint her again. (I don't know what she wanted from me. I never do.) Now, she just needed to occupy the span of time it would take to drink her drink before she could leave.

It had been a kind of gift, she said, the absence of office life, even the reduction in income and therefore in spending, and the general social slowdown. Her husband had decided to stay in Malaysia, she said, where he was working on a case involving a toxic paint plant causing birth defects. She had the whole house to herself, she and her cat, Fixx, whom her husband didn't like anyway. I'm trying to keep things straight. Her husband had made it clear that she shouldn't worry about *pulling her weight*—he had never understood her hanging on to a job she could take or leave—and she was coming to share his view.

I was rocking just a little on my stool as Celia talked.

Rocking is a little like nodding, and nodding is not unusual when talking with a friend. It felt good to rock, or to nod. It felt good to be sitting on the stool.

She felt guilty, she said, playing with her cocktail napkin, bunching it up and then smoothing it out again. But she was trying to make up for her good fortune by checking in regularly on the people in her life who had less, or who had nobody.

Celia looked at me when she said this, and I looked back at her. Oh.

She thinks I have nothing, nobody. She doesn't

know about my project. She doesn't know about Tala; she has made it clear she doesn't want to know.

I smiled at her then, meekly and gratefully. I stopped nodding completely. I sat up so straight! I am an actor, after all.

This seemed to be what Celia needed; I saw her face relax. Her face was like the face of a middle manager at the end of a staff meeting in which whatever the manager said has made the employees feel better, or at least made them feel less revolted or less abused. *They don't hate me. I'm not a bad person*, the face said. *Look how it's possible for the world to be made whole.*

Celia then seemed to decide that what was needed was a continuation of this lively one-sided conversation in which she went into more detail about her last few months' activities, the trajectory of her work, the health and habits of Fixx, the news she had accumulated about people I didn't know personally but who were mildly famous and therefore presumably of interest to all. This conversation didn't ask much of me, so I didn't give it much, and instead I cast my eyes around the bar.

In the corner booth: a group of young people playing some kind of tabletop game, concentrating, wearing blank expressions that could be mistaken—you would be mistaken—for boredom.

At a tall bar table: a person seated on the high chair,

with another person standing close, stroking the first person's short auburn hair.

At the barstool behind Celia: an old person with watery eyes and skin so pale it looked almost blue, left hand around a pint of beer and right hand tapping the table lightly, in time to the Velvet Underground.

Walking in the door, a middle-aged person with darker skin, a studied hairdo and designer workwear, pausing, eyes adjusting to the dark, then scanning the room for someone.

The ground jerked without warning and didn't stop. Massive, roiling movements, I wanted my cane from the floor, tried to hook it onto my foot to bring it within reach of my hand, finally succeeded on the fourth or fifth try, Celia was talking on about her painting, her cat, but the whole place was shaking as if dynamite had exploded deep underground and the shock waves were only just beginning to reach us on the surface, I lurched for her arm, she was speaking, her pacified expression cut now with frank annoyance, and the door blew in then, hitting the middle-aged designer-workwear person in the back of the head, in the back of that studied hairdo, and I grabbed Celia's hand, which she yanked away, and with the help of my cane I climbed off the chair without falling and staggered from one point of relative stability to the next—high chair, booth back, door frame—and made it out to the street, now dark except for a few dim streetlights, and empty except for the parked cars that I now stumbled between, leaning on each for as long as was necessary to regain my balance before striking out again on the buckled pavement, which was still moving, ever more blanketed by that fine, beige sand.

pirouettes are social, learned
ungrounded is carrying forward or a telling off
and if I refuse the medium /
and if the medium comes / despite /
what bargains are ever forgiven by the coin
my friends, my friends, my fertile friends
to abhor without loving—love without—

IV.

IT'S STRANGE TO be sleeping in this room again. I wake up every morning after visiting the past.

The nature of the visits can be sweet or sour, sometimes I wake slowly and want nothing but to go back down, back into some vague prior realm, webbed in indistinct, platonic love (we marched in the streets, we cooked and ate in droves, we danced); other times I wake with a jump and put my hand to my blazing cheek. Those face-flushed mornings are unbearable. Tala is present in both kinds of dreams, of course. But in the bad ones she mocks me, while in the good ones she's there by my side.

Then I check my messages, my bank account. There are no messages. The bank account is draining, slowly. I get to work.

Once, crouched among boxes and crates in a self-storage unit, I was shown a box of notebooks and left alone with them for hours. I was told the notebooks were the work of a young composer, and that she called them her *self-analysis*—they were different colors and dimensions, and bore handwritten titles that named various axes of musical theory or compositional practice.

Volume. Tone. Timbre. Meter. Pitch.

I leafed through them. They were filled with indecipherable diagrams and incomprehensible performance scores. Dots and lines, curves, shapes, words; words that had been crossed out; letters that clearly stood for things, for actions or emphases or tones. Acronyms, underlined twice. Circuits or what might have been circuits. Blots.

I couldn't understand any of it, really, despite my not-insignificant training in music. But I understood something of what it meant, something of its disobedience. In one notebook I found a sentence that felt like an instruction. I retyped it at my desk after copying it, in the self-storage room, by hand on the back of a receipt. The sentence remains, years later, magneted to my refrigerator door: GET OUT OF THE INSTRU-MENT A TIMBRE, (AND CONTINUE TO PLAY, i.e., EXPLORE MORE SPECIFICALLY THE COL-LECTION OF FREQUENCY CHARACTERIS-TICS WITHIN THIS TIMBRE).

The largest of the notebooks was thick and black and it was titled Outer Space.

I think she called them *composition books*, actually. Which makes sense, as she was a composer.

My own work, which will culminate in the completion of my project to eliminate Tala, must begin with my own version of *self-analysis*. With my own stack of note-books that I can carry from the bedroom to the living room, to the kitchenette, and back. In various sizes, col-ors, and shapes: an array. In which I can *take down* what I know, what I don't know, and what I need to unlearn, on a variety of different fronts.

To unknow, you must inventory what has been forced upon you. Inside you. What you shoved in, or al-lowed to be shoved in. The cock-sentences, word cocks. The countless invasions. You must inventory what you learned, what you never wanted to learn.

My notebooks are a *stroke of luck*, they are a *sign of the times*. If the ground had not started to move, I would never have had the *spare time* necessary to keep them. I would not be on furlough, and I would not be receiving *relief,* enough to get by *for the time being.* The first notebook addresses this: it's titled On Having to Have a Job.

The composer, when she commenced her process of self-analysis, would have been about Tala's age. She was a prodigy, and a success. But she didn't obey; she veered. She chose her composition books. She chose to see where they would lead.

Who was it who looked at the composer, who was it who saw her? What enabled her disobedience? What was the cost? I don't have the composer's confidence. Or Tala's. But I have something, don't I? Mustn't I? Maybe all I have is a lack of boundaries, a lack of obedience to boundaries.

No borders, we would chant. No nations.

Not even the nation of the self. Especially not that.

I wonder: Do you imagine what I am imagining, when I imagine destroying her for good?

GET OUT OF the instrument a timbre, and explore the collection of frequency characteristics within this timbre.

It's easy to stare at a sentence until the sentence becomes something else. It's like staring at a sunrise in the desert, or anywhere you can look at a sunrise and read it through to the end. First the sharp edge of a mountain, like a broken-off stone. A deep color between purple and brown. Above that, some kind of pale green-blue streaked with ivory. Or yellow.

How the colors *ivory* and *yellow* border each other, but the words could not be more distinct.

Next and above, the oranges and reds, lined with indigo and violet if there are clouds, a red-orange-indigo into the pale blue they call *robin's egg*, which turns the purple green. The light moves up but the colors move down; this is what mesmerizes. The *fingers* can be *rosy*; this makes us ancient.

Then the mountain grass turns mauve and the sand blushes for a minute, the whole scene blushes for a minute, you can't look away, you'll miss a second, which is to miss a word. Then, the blue bruise to cover up the blush, the embarrassment. Blue of vein, blue of return. Follow the fingers and there's nothing but that rose of blush, nothing but that bruise of consequence. How they wash each other out, a *marriage made in heaven*.

And all of this happens and must be interpreted, all of this happens and must be explained, named. An eternity before the actual sun appears. Before the actual appearance, the actual revelation of the nameable. Of the narrative, of the actual first cause. *Actual*: a word that has always been set in time.

When it does appear, that cause, that sun, its effects fade instantly. The bruise gives way to a blank clear blue, to the light of day; it is good, we are told, the sun is *up* and the day is good. Everything that led up to that blank clear blue is over, is *history*. The sun is nothing but brightness, and brightness is nothing but goodness, and goodness is above all blank.

The good blank brightness is all you will know, is all you are told if you don't happen upon its making, if you don't happen upon the right scene at the right time. If you don't get there first and catch it in the act.

It's easy to stare at a sentence and start repeating it in your mind. When the sentence is an invitation to explore, then to read the sentence is to leave the sentence. To veer.

Get out of the instrument a timbre. I was taught to take my body as an instrument, and to take the world as its text. *Timbre*: the quality given to a sound by its overtones. When I explore the sentence about timbre I find myself *veering*—as if being pulled, *trained*—along axes that don't relate to composition or to music at all, but that do relate to time. As in saying "I was taught."

One-half of my family—the big half, the populous half—suffered greatly in the last century, in an unfamous sequence of events: of occupation, civil war, famine, dictatorship, and struggle to survive. It's strange how some sequences of episodes become internationally famous, become *part of the fabric* of our shared social consciousness, while some recede into backstories, appearing when sought for in books and on screens, but not already there in the collective imagination as a *matter of course*. Not beyond the borders of their occurrence, that is. Or the bodies that crossed them.

The sequences are alive and yet they languish, visible and not. This is a dissonance.

I was taught that dissonance and timbre are inextricably related. That dissonance is the opposite of consonance, and that consonance is a "pleasant instance" of timbre. I was taught that consonance is defined by "the feeling of stability and well-being that is produced when two tones are played simultaneously." The way to tell if something was consonant or dissonant was to pay attention to how a pair of notes, when played together, *made you feel*. I was taught that this method of definition through experience both was and was not provable, scientifically. That the practice both did and did not produce scientific fact.

For the families that survived or partially survived those unfamous sequences of world events, the aliveness of the events in the imaginations of individuals varies. But the aliveness, in some form or other, is nonetheless present in the survivors and in the survivors of the survivors— whether or not their heads were filled with images from the scenes that made up the events. Scenes of what? Of sibling fighting sibling, of homes shot with international bullets, stormed by international soldiers. Of illness, of the effects of famine and malnutrition, of eating things that are not meant to be food. Of eyes failing, teeth failing, growth halted mid-spurt. Of the starved-to-death multiplying on unpaved, unmarked streets. And whether or not these scenes are shared explicitly with the survivors of the survivors—especially if they were brought to live far away, by choice or by force, or by some combination thereof—the survivors of these survivors, and their survivors too, will feel their effects.

But first, an eternity spent imagining that good blank brightness. Practicing to make it real.

Maybe this is all there is to know or to ask. What are the effects of events on the beings who bear them?

I am of course an example, a child and a grandchild of one of those families. Survivor of a survivor. A once-removed product of an unfamous sequence of events.

So is Tala. I know it without her having to say it aloud.

THE DAYS ARE getting longer, though it's not yet spring. It gives me the impression of having more time, which in turn makes me feel a responsibility to use that time, to *make it count.*

I don't want to go outside every day. It's too confusing; I can't speak to people the way I once could. It's as if there is a film between me and everyone else. The film is like a bubble and it's also like a screen. The movie is playing backward.

But at the same time, I'm in love with the outside. I'm getting better at walking through the chaos of upheavals. Sometimes I wonder if I would even know anymore how to walk on a flat surface, one with no chance of suddenly convulsing.

I imagine it would be like the sensation of stepping off a treadmill or people mover, but over and over again, endlessly. Never readjusting to *the status quo.*

J.P. IS COMING over. His text this morning prompted me to return to the glossy white brochure. I held it, turned it over, tried to force my thoughts to *gather*.

Something had been nagging me about it, about that series of questions I partially answered before tossing the thing into a drawer. Now, the work I've begun doing in my notebooks has helped me understand what the nagging thing might be.

What kept me in acting classes and middle school plays was the homework, the mimeographed assignments meant to assist in "character development." My first Theater Arts teacher sent us home with a scene to study, and a worksheet with a list of questions (I would have been eleven):

—What does your character want from this scene?

—How does any preexisting relationship between your character and your scene partner's character affect your character's expectations when entering the scene?

— What did your character eat for breakfast?

— What is he most afraid of?

— What makes her feel safe?

By high school, the mimeographed pages gave way to xeroxed ones listing, instead of questions, "strategies." This was a different teacher, one who believed his role was parental, paternal: to produce as many professional actors as he could. He succeeded, but at a cost (to him, to us—to his own children, I imagine, though I never learned if this was true).

The strategies included:

— Gather as much detail as possible about your character and saturate your environment with depictions of the details. Plaster your walls with images of your character's house, clothes, dreams.

— Listen to his music, use the shampoo he would use and wear the perfume she would wear. Throw your own stuff out, or hide it from view.

— Speak in your character's voice as you go about your day.

— Remember that total immersion will lead

to success, and that anything less will result in failure.
—Trust the method.

I don't know, or can't recall, if anyone else obeyed the
instruction to swap out their stuff. I did, every time I
got a part. And I always got a part. As a result, I never
had a favorite shirt, or a favorite song, or a favorite color.
I also never had a lot of stuff.

(We didn't know what this "method" was, then,
only that we were to trust it.)

And now? I sense myself at the mercy of I-don't-
know-what. The movie plays backward and forward at
the same time.

I titled my second notebook On Being the Student.

When he arrived, barging in without knocking, swinging his long arms around, J.P. asked if he could look
through my food and supplies, and started opening
cabinet doors before I could reply. He and his collaborators have set up a drop-off spot for durable and per-
ishable goods, the location of which has been spread
by word of mouth to the least fortunate of those who
live unofficial lives, and who therefore aren't eligi-
ble for the various forms of bureaucratic relief—as

paltry as they are—that are keeping the rest of us afloat.

I let him have a few cans of beans, three bars of soap, a bundle of mismatched socks. Twelve boxes of tampons, representing the last year of the lifetime supply that had been an extra perk from my most lucrative commercial. (A year since I've used them, a year since I wondered, "Is a *lifetime* over when one no longer has a use for tampons?" but did nothing to cancel the supply.) The bedroom closet had become a jumble of Tala's clothes and mine. I pulled out an equal number of garments belonging to us each. One of hers, one of mine, one of hers, one of mine. By the time he left, J.P. had stuffed his giant messenger bag so completely, we had to tie it shut with twine.

I stopped him on his way out. "I filled in that brochure," I said, "but only out of curiosity, as research." I handed it to him, stamped and addressed. He looked at it like he'd never seen it before. "Can you mail it off for me?" He shrugged, took it out of my hand, and left. A violent aftershock followed his departure, knocking me to the floor. Later, I wrote on the first page of On Being the Student:

"FIRST LESSON: The authority of other people always supersedes mine, even when it comes to my own experience. I look elsewhere for information about myself."

Before he left, while we were packing up the clothing and sundries into his bag, I asked J.P. how he keeps his balance out there. He repeated the words, or if not exactly the words then at least the sentiment, of the Breton sailor: balance begins and ends with the gut. He jumped up from his chair and stood facing me, legs and arms slightly bent, tense. Then pounded his belly so I could hear the resistance of his abdominals: *rock hard.* "They can't move me," he said, stuck out his tongue, and sat back down.

WAKING UP ON the floor hours later, light almost gone, holding a pen in one hand and On Being a Student in the other.

Waking up with a terrible desire to see Tala, with such a painful longing I sat without moving for what felt like an hour, unable to grasp what time it was or where I had been, able only to gaze up at the door and to picture her—involuntarily, the pictures just play on their own—coming up the alley in her black ankle boots. Able only to listen for her key in the lock, to softly call out her name.

It was a longing that felt like lust, but wasn't, that felt like envy but wasn't. There was pity, too, and fear (of contamination maybe, though not knowing what that might mean). I look for labels, for something to write down, to keep. But labels are distractions from such floods of feeling, are no more help than the illustrations of pain spectra hanging in doctor's offices waiting for a wavering finger to point to some cartoon face that is supposed to describe what a body is experiencing. It turns out certain forms of pain are compounded by their lack of an accurate label, by their resistance to description. (It turns out I'm an expert in these forms.)

I was having these thoughts, in language, as I was experiencing the incapacities of that language, which is when pain erupts. So I was crying, too, first softly then violently, and soon also rocking back and forth, a rocking that was more of a nodding of the entire upper half of my body—*keening*—like a professional mourner, or like a child in the final phase of their tantrum.

The keening transported me back to fourth-period Fundamentals of Acting, to the teacher who minted professionals (my picture hangs in the auditorium's green room, I'm told).

To elaborate: while I was rocking, while I was keening in the wake of my disorienting nap (which followed upon J.P.'s disorienting visit), I was experiencing actual distress but I was also experiencing the awareness of a dissonance between my body's actions and my psychological state.

I was not only responding to the present disorienting moment but was also reliving a past experience of intense emotion. My present actions were being affected by this reliving of the past, which meant—this occurred to me even as I rocked and keened, keened and rocked—that in some sense, that *for all intents and purposes*, what I was doing was equivalent to an exercise, that what I was doing was equivalent to practicing my technique. (I was doing all of this while still sitting on the floor by the daybed, the light almost gone.)

The specific past experience I was reliving was one from those years long ago, from school. It was a scene of me and my classmates, each performing the Affective Memory exercise simultaneously, scattered on the high school auditorium stage facing in different directions, each of us engaged, as instructed, in a memory of an *acute trauma*. Our task was to *let arise* the associated sounds, gestures, facial expressions, while the teacher (Coach X, we were to call him—his name was Xander) walked around yelling "What did you hear? Hear it! What did you smell? Smell it!" and the scene I had chosen to replay in my mind—which might be too personal, too trivial, and too embarrassing even to be transcribed into On Being the Student—had brought me to a state similar to the one I found myself in now, a state of rocking and keening and wailing, and on that day in the auditorium as Coach X egged us on, on one of the upward swings of my keening's rise and fall, I caught a glimpse (unintentionally, and disobediently) of my friend Veronica, who was herself also keening and wailing, whose eyes did not meet mine.

(I only learned years later to name this exercise Affective Memory, or to know anything of its origins. My classmates and I were led—by omission, but still led— to believe that Coach X was the sole originator of it, as of every *trick to his trade*, every *tool in his box*.)

Because Veronica was my friend, I knew that her

stepmother, a woman she had loved and who adored her, had died of a sudden aneurism two weeks before. I wasn't the only one who knew this, it was common knowledge, but I may have known more than the others—certainly more than Coach X—how genuine her grief was, since at that time it was never assumed that stepparents were beloved. And my knowledge of Veronica's outsized grief as compared to the dubious, inconsequential grief I was working so hard to summon—both of them leading to outwardly identical manifestations (which received identical levels of praise from Coach X)—the dissonance between our two claims to grief—led to its own trauma, the trauma of comparison, and it was this trauma I was now reliving, on the floor of my living room, between the daybed and the kitchenette, as my upper body swayed up and down, hinged at the waist, and my throat bled out an anguished wail, mourning an anticipated loss that I couldn't know (without confirmation from Tala that she was gone forever), that I couldn't be certain was even real. Grief added to grief, dissonance added to dissonance, no way out, no way in. No mask when everything is mask. Scratch an actor and you'll find, et cetera.

"My project, my project, my project," I chanted in a whisper, after sound had had enough of me. Come back to the breath. Come back into the room.

IT IS A luxury to be vulnerable in performance. I have managed it, here and there, when there were enough protections, or when the stakes were comparatively low. You too may have seen the documentary about the making of *The Shining*, seen the freedom Jack Nicholson has that Shelley Duvall doesn't share: how he rants and flails between takes—protected, perhaps, by his Method—while she, panicked on the floor, draped in the coats of crew members with conscience, falls apart. (Shelley Duvall! A genius, whose life should win an Academy Award.)

Is it a luxury to be vulnerable, or is it a right? *When did you stop? / What would it take for you to do it again?* Is it a luxury to be vulnerable and expect to survive *in one piece*?

I have to go outside. As soon as the intention forms in my consciousness, the ground moves again, slow and steady but also intense, just like the keening was. As far as I know, despite her talent Veronica did not become a *professional*. She did a few plays in college and then went into something technological and remunerative. This is the first time I've thought about her in years, decades. We were friends.

The ground keeps moving, undulating, and I give in to it, lie down on my back, drape my sweater over my chest.

Tomorrow I'll go out. For now, pity me. Cover me in coats.

> *difference of kind, difference of degree*
> *prank calls to god (nothing happens)*
> *finishing a thought is a finishing off*
> *when every surface has been touched*
> *go and ask for the real thing, simple*
> *syrup over a slow fire. it's only nonsense*
> *if you let it—bitters—come and see.*

V.

I TITLED MY third notebook Volume, or, Varieties of Involuntary Audio Experience. I began it from a need—sudden, urgent, to make sense of an experience from my past. It was not a success: the notebook is full of crossed-out phrases, sentences that lead nowhere. Where I have failed in my notebook, I will attempt, here, to explain.

I once tried to get a temp job at a legal firm for which the main qualification, according to the posting, was "outstanding reading speed and comprehension."

Actors are practiced at this. The "cold read" of a

script at an audition is essentially a speed read, followed by an interpretation, followed by a performance, and both the speed read and the interpretation need to happen so quickly as to go unnoticed. I filled in the application and named two recent directors as references, and I was called for an interview, where they gave me and a room full of other finalists a test: a twenty-page legal brief, followed by a multiple-choice quiz. The firm was looking for several people, they explained, to go through a mountain of files for an intricate case. This reading assessment alone—no interrogation, no references—would determine which and how many of us they'd take on: they were looking for a combined score of 85 percent comprehension with a speed of eight hundred words per minute.

On my way out, the HR person who had administered the test took me aside to deliver my results: "One hundred, four hundred," the HR person said, "comprehension over speed. If I may . . ."—here there was a dropped voice, a softened delivery—"I'm betting you're an auditory reader, so you'll never break four hundred—it's like breaking the sound barrier. You did well, though." Did the HR person pat me on the back as I left? I don't remember, but it's possible. I did not get the job.

I looked up "auditory reader" and easily recognized myself.

Yes, reading for me meant hearing each word in my head; yes, anytime I tried to pick up speed, after a point I would start to feel psychically tongue-tied: desynchronized, tripped up, and eventually stalled by my silent voice's inability to keep up with my mind's appetite.

I did more research. I learned that accomplished speed readers like John F. Kennedy (everybody's favorite example, it seemed)—but also ordinary faster-than-normal readers—are said to pass over this thing people like me do, "subvocalization," altogether. That they read by way of—and this made no sense to me then, nor does it now—"direct absorption through the eyes." (Elsewhere, this was described as "like gleaning information from a picture," which at least was a metaphor I could understand.) Perhaps for no reason except that I was used to understanding my body as my instrument and tool, and therefore under my control, I resented this newly identified limitation. I didn't want to be an auditory reader, slow and burdened by uninvited sound. I wanted speed: one hundred over eight hundred, at least. I wanted what these super readers had.

After losing the legal job I was hired elsewhere, as an overnight proofreader at a sports magazine. Now that I had work, I embarked on an attempt to eliminate what I had come to think of as the silent voice that lived in my mouth. (This must have been during the period when I was studying *The Shining*—studying, that is, the genius of Shelley Duvall—in which the boy, Danny, Duvall's movie son, called the voice that only he could hear "the little boy that lives in my mouth.")

I practiced this elimination for a month. I practiced at work, on the sports articles, but soon recognized that even nonauditory readers might find themselves sounding out words when they had been hired specifically to look for mistakes. I practiced on scripts, where it seemed like too much to ask, given that scripts are meant to be spoken aloud. I practiced on newspapers and blogs and street signs and billboards and product labels and novels. I would start by looking at a sentence or a paragraph and focusing on the visual appearance of the words, as if on the characters of an unfamiliar alphabet. I would describe the shapes of the letters, a curve here, a descending line, a dot. The more I looked at the words in this way, and then at the groups of words that made phrases, brand names, sentences, the more presence they seemed to have. Like little creatures, independent entities. Glyphs. At first I congratulated myself that I was already transitioning, that I was becoming a visual reader.

But this purposeful defamiliarization was not, it turned out, the thing I was trying to learn. When I tried to re-create the conditions of the test and beat my score of four hundred words per minute—first counting the number of words on a page, and then setting a stopwatch for the page's completion—not only did I still hear the voice pronouncing any words my scanning eyes couldn't help but pause on (because, inevitably, they paused), I also understood nothing of the text before me. Just scrambled signs in all directions, and a headache for my efforts.

After that month, I entered an attentive period, in which I became hyperaware of the frequency with which my silent voice accompanied my every mental action. I began to wonder if I was the only person who heard every thought pronounced, in their voice, in their head. Because it was always recognizably my voice, I didn't worry that I was *losing my mind*, or *hearing voices*, or *cracking up*. I began to wonder if this experience of constant self-narration was less universal than I'd always, without ever explicitly considering it, assumed.

What if all, or even half, the people in the world weren't walking around with a headful of language all the time? What if all, or even half, the people I *knew* weren't?

What if, whenever I was truly baffled by someone's— a lover's, or a friend's, or a celebrity's—report of their inner experience ("What are you thinking?" "Nothing."), the explanation was not that they were withholding, or that somehow they didn't have an inner life at all, but that their inner life was not reportable the way mine was, because it wasn't happening in words?

Though it was my voice in the sense that it did not sound like somebody else's voice, it was also not my voice, in that it often said things I would not say aloud, and sometimes things I would not have thought I would think. Whereas the little voice that lives inside Danny's mouth doesn't speak in Danny's voice but in a squashed, constricted tone that is irritating to hear, and it also has a name that is different from Danny's: Tony. (Mine has not introduced itself.) Apparently in the book, it's revealed at some point that the voice is that of Danny's adult self, traveling backward in time to warn his younger version of a multitude of dangers, and revelations, to come. In the movie version, no such explanation is put forth. I have not read the book.

I think I am already too old for the voice in my silent mouth to represent an older version of myself; plus, as I said, it sounds (if *sounds* is the right word) just like me.

I SAID I would go outside, and I did.

The voice that is mine and not mine, though it sounds just like me, chanted all the way from the alley behind my patio, along the wide and vacant avenue, across the overpass above the school bus purgatory, and into the maze of narrower, building-shaded streets called Center City.

It chanted, *And what will you do if you find her, really?* and *What if there's another way?* It chanted, *What would it take for you to do it again?* It chanted, *Innerwelt, Umwelt, Innerwelt, Umwelt,* two words I didn't know but that I had seen written as graffiti, on the side of the alley dumpster after my flight from that stage—a lifetime ago, if only a stone's throw away. Then for the length of ten city blocks it chanted, *Strangers, subjects, locale, mood, voice.* It seemed to be chanting in time with my halting gait, keeping tempo with my cane.

The building associated with Box 6532, Center City—which, I found out from a records database I still have access to from my dormant job, was located at the far edge of that district, on a short, curved alley otherwise devoid of functioning businesses—was nondescript, with a sign above the door that displayed a symbol but no words, no brand or corporate name. The symbol looked vaguely like a hook, though it might have been a *J*. The door was locked, but the lights were on.

Inside, behind the deeply tinted windows, I could just make out a stereotypical office scene, though it also resembled a provisional base for a local election: cheap, semi-cubicled desks lining one edge, whiteboards on the opposite wall, one of those easels with a giant paper pad propped up near the whiteboards, a row of folding chairs lined up in a rolling rack parked in a corner, all beneath a grid of overhead fluorescent lights. There were people, maybe eight or ten of them, sitting at the desks and talking on headsets, or standing in urgent conversation in the empty center of the room. Regular people, different enough from one another not to cohere into a single demographic, but similar enough—all dressed as if from the cheap side of the mall—to seem connected by something other than happenstance.

None of them looked like Tala (none of them was Tala).

The lights cast a greenish tinge, which, combined with the tint of the window, made the whole scene feel underwater, or radioactive. At one point, as I looked at the window, as I tried to absorb the whole meaning of its text with my eyes, I saw in it a repeating pattern of glossy green leaves.

I looked for a bell or intercom but saw none. I knocked on the glass and was surprised by its solidity. Nobody looked up. I turned around, sensing I was being watched from behind. The alley was quiet; a light coating of sand swirled on the asphalt and narrow sidewalk. I began to wave at the office workers inside, first with a small motion and then a more energetic one. I yelled, "Hello!" I began to jump up and down while continuing to wave and yell, but my feet when they landed were met with a giant tremor that knocked me to the ground.

There is a period of recovery after a fall, a moment of reorientation, while the earth continues to pulse but the danger as such has passed, and in these moments my powers of perception are especially acute. From my perch on the ground I was able to recognize that the building's facade was in fact a one-way mirror, but that unlike those of some banks and other ground-floor establishments on busier streets and avenues, this mirror faced inward—giving the street side the view, and keeping the workers, the people inside the office, in the dark. As if I were in the witness position, and they were the suspects.

And I was able to notice a clear plastic box on the ground at the right side of the door. A slotted box for *literature* (Take one!) which would normally have been hung from a wall or a door but seemed to have fallen, maybe due to the tremors. It lay on its side, and it appeared to still have some *literature* inside. I pulled myself up with my cane and went over to it, stooped down and extracted a couple of postcard-size cards, which I put into my coat pocket.

The scene inside the office continued, unaware of my presence, like an animated diorama or a surveillance tape. Two of the people who had been talking earnestly in the center of the room were now cinched in a hug.

AT THE BAR, I reclaimed the spot where I'd waited for Celia the last time.

It was fuller today, which surprised me since it was also earlier, afternoon—is the whole city on furlough? I was lucky to find my familiar stool empty. I'm not sure I would have stayed if I hadn't.

This time, I hung my cane next to my coat on the under-bar hooks. I ordered a beer from the gruff bartender—not the same one as before. The crowd rumbled and hissed around me, most of its chatter combining with the music to produce a mid-to-high-volume white noise. Dial turned to 8. But as always, when I was alone and not focused on something compelling enough to block them out, the voices came through, intermittent but unmistakable. Like listening to an FM station at the edge of its range.

A high, honey voice said, "Impractical, right? But he insists it makes total sense!"

A low, gravel voice said, laughing, "*Lis*ten, I'm *try*ing."

An even lower voice, deliberate and drawn out, said, "Never . . . fucking . . . again . . . I . . . do . . . not . . .

lie," and then let out an exaggerated sigh. Then a small mercy: a couple sat to my left and began speaking rapidly in a language I don't know. I swiveled toward them to increase the volume of their voices over the rest. The relief was instant.

I pulled out one of the cards I'd stashed in my coat pocket. White type on a black ground, in the same bold typeface J.P.'s glossy brochure had used:

ANXIETY IS THE EXPERIENCE OF THE FACT THAT THE WHOLE SOCIAL ORDER AND ALL OF SCIENCE IS AN ARBITRARY AND UNGROUNDED CONSENSUS. THERE IS NO SOLID SELF AND NO BRUTE FACTS. NO WAY TO MAKE SENSE OF AND BE AT HOME IN THE WORLD.

Something was tapping against my right shoulder in rhythmic intervals, tap tap tap tap tap. I heard the sound of a stool dragging on the bar floor, and the rhythmic tapping stopped.

I turned the card over. On this side, the ground was white and the type, huge and black, read "ANXIETY = TRUTH," and, in smaller letters below it, "Set Yourself Free." The only other marking on the card was that same, odd logo that resembled a hook or a hand-drawn, awkward *J*.

Turning this card over in my hand and rereading its message, I felt such an instant and penetrating hopelessness I could barely resist putting my head on the bar and succumbing to it. But I knew that such a move would get me ejected: it had happened before. So I resisted.

I read and reread the words. Soon, they were picked up by the voice inside my silent mouth and gathered force: an army of words weaponized by the silent voice, conquering my tongue's will. The phrases *Anxiety is the experience of the fact* and *There is no solid self* and *No way to make sense*, and some single words like *ungrounded* and *home*, pounded at each other in a violent round, a vagrant fugue, and I tried to hold my mouth shut so as not to let them out, and also so as not to talk back. Two different battles, difficult in two different ways.

I put my hands to my temples and gave my head a shake, and the chorus died back a little. I opened my mouth and delivered, in the direction of the gruff bartender, my leaving script. The thing I had practiced, that I knew would get me by. "What do I owe?"

It isn't that there are no other bars in Center City. It's that I don't know of any others Tala is likely to go to. I don't know which ones are open in these conditions, and I don't know how far I can walk without risking getting stranded, unable to make it home.

Besides, I was deflated; I'd had hope. But there wasn't the faintest scent of Tala there.

LUCID. THERE IS something I know. It's about the message on the card. The one about selves, facts, anxiety, and home.

A knowledge that has been submerged for many years, or that had been broken down (by time? or by time and something else?) into such small particles of memory-information, it has passed through the plasma membrane—that which separates *interior* from environment—of thousands, of millions of my cells. Passed through to the other side, to the in-side.

I imagine these particles of memory-information crossing over from environment to interior, and in crossing over, becoming something else. Becoming self, no longer subjects of study, or of scrutiny. If only we could look inside ourselves, really look! Without externalization, without fiction or projection. I have wished for this for so long. For a diagnostic needle or a psychic laparoscope.

The thing I know about the message on the card I know with the simple kind of knowledge that comes from recognition. I recognized the words.

They had been spoken to me once—to me and to

many others—by a dead professor of the Theory of Drama, in an attempt to personalize the obscure expression of a thinker he revered. The professor was alive at the time, and it may be that the words were written, not spoken, since the professor communicated to me and to the others in both ways.

However it was transmitted, the message was clear: Most people live inauthentically, and to live authentically one must pass through a state of anxiety. Not pass through—*dwell in*. The professor was gentle, it must be said, and full of joy (joy was, we were told, a by-product of the anxious state).

Still, the gentle professor admitted that the thinker whom he revered never quite worked out an account of how a life, how any individual life, could *mean*.

I took out another notebook, a fourth, and titled it The Gentle Professor.

IT'S HAPPENED AGAIN. I haven't left home in days.

I'd hardly left this room until a stretch of cloudless mornings arrived, creating the conditions for a sudden and violent attack of the sun's rays on my face at approximately 9:10 a.m. Now I may be compelled to move back to the living room, the daybed. Not that the difference is very big.

Strange how language encapsulates time. And power, and relation. I don't know when or where I first heard the phrase *create the conditions*, and yet when I hear myself pronounce it, either out loud or in my silent mouth, I am aware of its age in my body, of how long it has been since it became mine. The phrase *create the conditions*—alongside many other phrases, some mundane (*create a space for*) and some more technical (*being thrown, always already*)—dates, in my body and in my silent mouth, to a specific time, the time I spent, along with other students of drama, of its *practice* and its *theory*, in the thrall of the gentle professor.

Maybe the phrases did not become mine. Maybe I became theirs.

And what if we could cross the membrane and look inside. Maybe then seekers wouldn't need therapists or cults, bosses wouldn't need one-way mirrors. Maybe then, actors wouldn't need a Method.

The mirrored windows at the office in the alley in Center City reminded me of the existence of mirrors. Looking glasses.

I rarely look in mine, but this morning after the sun forced me out of bed I took a long stare at myself in the cheap plastic mirror mounted to the inside of the closet door. My self was there, looking back at me. I raised up a hand and watched my self do the same. Just to be sure, I placed both of my hands on both of my throats.

What is left of me is visible in the mirrored glass. I am not a natural beauty. I am too old to have the beauty of youth and I am too stupid to have the beauty of wisdom and I am too unkind or at least not demonstratively kind enough to have what is called "inner beauty." If I possess anything, it is the glamour of a performer, which is not beauty, but it is something.

What is left for the performer who no longer performs?

I have been dreaming, these nights, about nonconsensual sex. I don't need to go into detail about it: they're my dreams, so I don't find them distressing, even when they shock me, which at times they do. They can shock me the way playing a part unlike "myself" can shock me: how natural it can feel, how un-false. How much of myself can only be expressed when I am *not myself.*

But dreaming is not done for an audience.

It isn't always true that listening to someone else describe their dream is boring. It's only true most of the time, because most of the time we don't really want to know other people. But when you're falling in love, when you're still vulnerable and toppling into the un-known, or when things are coming apart at the end of love, you want nothing more than to know your be-loved's dreams. You seek the meaning within them like in a crystal ball. The rest of the time, dreaming is a code we keep secret even from ourselves.

At some point I accepted as fact a theory I read once: it claimed that dreams take the experiences from our lives and disassemble them, then neutralize them through recombination. Through making them into new stories, like a montage of the scraps that would otherwise be left on a cutting-room floor. (I don't know whose metaphor this is. Maybe it's mine.)

The important thing is that the new stories don't always displace the old ones, they just reduce their authority. They de-authorize them. By confusing the signal, the new stories can at least partially cancel the old ones out. The important thing is—according to my memory, though of course neither my memory nor the theory is sure to be trustworthy—that it doesn't seem to matter if the new stories are, themselves, equally disturbing, or even if they are more disturbing than the experienced events they are attempting to replace. Their role isn't to lighten things up; the work they do is only the work of dis-attachment, of insisting on multiplicity.

J.P. went through a phase of preaching *obfuscation* as a countersurveillance technique. Flood the field with competing targets, he would say, and you can make yourself disappear.

Not all stories are bombs, but some of them are. If your story is a bomb, then a dream can defuse it. Then it can disassemble it, and then it can disappear it via the repurposing of its parts.

So many junk metaphors are military. So many images fill language full of war.

Reduce the bomb to acetone, hydrogen peroxide, and finishing nails. Turn it into a fresh manicure, a clean counter, a picture hung above a fire.

None of this matters, this dreaming, this thinking, unless it helps elucidate my project. (The word *transformation* is another that my body can date. It is the same age as the others. All of the terms that are *coming up* for me are the same age. *Coming up for* is another of those terms. The circle closes in. The ground responds with another shake.)

I WANT TO describe how it felt to meet Tala for the first time. Not what happened—I've already accounted for that—but how it felt.

Before the earth began its articulations, its regular convulsions, I had been uneasy for a long time. Since I was Tala's age, if not longer. I've explained some of this already. More of it is detailed in the notebooks, distributed across them according to subject, in charts and graphs as well as sentences and fragments scrawled in my imprecise hand. But the dreams about nonconsensual sex are stirring something, making me want to *go deeper*. (Is there a more junk metaphor than that?)

There is the question of how dreams come to be, and then there is the question of what we are to make of them. The people who concern themselves with these questions don't often compare notes.

For instance, it is convenient to believe that when people appear in dreams they are only symbols, not themselves. It is convenient, whether or not it is also true. This is why interpretations come out involuntarily when we narrate our dreams. Interpretations are to dreams what punchlines are to jokes—they're how we *get it*.

It seems to me that people and things in dreams are like actors in a play or a film, that they are simultaneously symbols and themselves. Stand-ins, parts-for-wholes. Not just people, things too, and situations. So when I dreamed, as I often did before furlough, of being late to my job, it was a dream about being late to my job. But it was also a dream about lateness, about ambivalence—I needed the job, I hated the job—about obedience and about resistance to that obedience.

My recurring dreams, leading up to my onstage disaster, leading up to Tala's arrival, were clichés. Being late, or unprepared for a meeting. Forgetting my lines on opening night. Forgetting my lines! Then Tala appeared: graceful, confident, beautiful, kind. Her whole life ahead of her. And, when I reflected these things back to her, when I noticed them aloud? Incapable of receiving them. *Don't judge another's outsides by your insides*—but outsides are also who we are, to everyone in the world. And the more unstable the outside is, the less possible it becomes to maintain any distinction at all. The membrane between grows thin. It was this thinness that I felt when addressing the witches from the stage, and that I felt again when Tala moved in.

I consider my current dreams about nonconsensual sex—which I should specify are primarily about consensual nonconsensual sex, though that edge will sometimes blur—to be an improvement, compared to the dreams of lateness and going up on my lines. Which means that some of what has happened since I met Tala has been necessary and good.

And yet I insist she must be eliminated. I don't know how I know it. I know it the way I know when I need to get up to empty my bladder, or how I know when I need to leave the house to avoid succumbing to a solipsistic, catatonic trance. I know it *in my bones.*

There is a lack of coherence in me right now, which creates an opening—a *space,* fine—or a *clearing,* whatever. Inside the incoherence is a new, bright coherence waiting to be seen. This is what the voice in my silent mouth tells me as I fall asleep.

> *sinking and singing, though underground*
> *fissures where relief gets processed*
> *if her hand is forced then everyone's is*
> *(fissures where the torture, too). don't try to*
> *   forget*
> *but then don't* make it whole, *how a figure*
> *   finds*
> *its ground, or how a finder maps its fall—*
> *you know it and you don't*

VI.

But I don't want her to kill herself, and I don't want her to vanish on her own. I need to be the one. I need to disappear her.

In the notebook titled Phantasy (the fifth notebook, small and with a bright-orange cover) I devote a section to imagining how Tala might be destroyed. There it is again, the passive mode, the tentative, the euphemistic. (Despite what I say, despite what I insist upon, I struggle to picture the murder—this act, my act. The section of the orange notebook will become a record of this struggle.)

———

As an actor, I have been asked to conjure murderous rage, murderous intent, on many an occasion. Not only against the stuffed goat, but against other people, other actors, sometimes ones so skilled, so committed, that the terror they are able to summon onstage as we play out the scene—the fake terror they are able to communicate as real; the real sweat that they have summoned with their fake terror; the performed panic that becomes real, physical panic; the hatred, the loss, the retreat and despair (the abandon, in some cases, and the defiance, in others)—becomes so *entwining*, so *enmeshing*, so *entraining* (the prefix *en-*, the gentle professor taught in a unit on the psychology of performance, means *within*), I crumble. *I* crumble, and what is left is something I can only call not-I. A luminous relief, a respite.

In what is left is the strength, the clarity, the courage to kill that which needs to be killed.

Recalling these experiences, conjuring this state, this not-I fills the pages of the orange notebook with scenarios, written out as scenes, complete with dialogue and blocking: Tala shot in the back from across a street; Tala, naked, drowned in the bath; Tala out the window, Tala under the bus; Tala strapped to a chair, a plastic bag over her beautiful head.

It pains me to describe these scenes so reductively.

It would pain me more to share them in full. They lack, among other things, imagination.

They lack, too, any clear view of my own presence on the scene (it is hard to imagine oneself). They are made up almost entirely of the dusty room, the angled lights, the shadowed wings—the presence of the stage.

COACH X PUT us through a number of *processes*. These I'm just beginning to remember. It's writing in the notebooks that is making me remember—that, and the cards that keep arriving at my door. I don't know who leaves them. J.P., perhaps. Or whoever it was who was watching me from the alley the other day when I stood there, transfixed by the workers in the office, with their cheap clothes and whiteboards and bear hugs.

The cards are all the same size, all black-and-white. Each presents a sentence or two on the front and a shorter equation or phrase on the back. The sentences jog my memory. Junk phrases. Things I learned without learning them. Things that entered through my cell walls. The voice in my silent mouth knows how to pronounce them on arrival. They clog me up.

THE RE-CREATION OF AN EXPERIENCE MAKES THE EXPERIENCE DISAPPEAR read the second card, and on its back: ANXIETY = THE DIZZINESS OF FREEDOM.

The third card that arrived was printed only on one side. It said: WHO WOULD BE WRONG IF YOUR LIFE BEGAN TO WORK? Turn it over: a blank, blank space.

The memories come so fast I can't copy them down in my notebooks without resorting to a shorthand even I won't be able to decipher.

The day Coach X made us name an "obstacle" to our "full emergence" as artists, and then brought us onstage to "reexperience" it. How Randy's obstacle was so unspeakable it took an hour to come out, and we never saw Randy again. ("He got what he needed," said Coach X. "I disappeared his obstacle, he became free, and he chose to leave.")

How he prepared the ground first by bringing Veronica onstage and making her headache disappear. "Where does it hurt?" "In my head." "Where in your head, you little brat!" "Behind my eyes." "Both eyes? Be precise! Get it, or I'll fail you!" "A half inch behind my left eye." "What kind of pain?" "It hurts!" "What kind of pain, are you an idiot or can you put two words together?" "Throbbing . . . pain!" "Good! Tell me how quickly it's throbbing now. How many throbs per second." "I don't know." "Well count them, goddamit! Count the throbs and describe your pain!" "I can't count them." "Well if you can't count them, can you say they exist?" "I have a—" "Have a? Or had a? *Do* you have a headache or *did* you have a headache?" "I have—I had. I don't know! I can't think!" "Damn right you can't think!

You've been too busy complaining about your headache. But now your headache's gone, isn't it? Didn't I make it disappear like I promised?" "You did, you made it . . . disappear . . ." "Good girl, now sit down and we'll move on to something interesting."

The scenes returned whole; I couldn't stop them. And on and on. From Coach X's after-school drama-club sessions, and from the gentle professor's class. Which one of them said what was written on the fourth card that appeared: LANGUAGE IS THE HOUSE OF BEING (on the back: GET IT / LOSE IT). I don't know. I can't remember. Maybe they both said it.

I go out. The ground is shaking. I don't find her. Again and again.

I need to change my tactic. I need to disappear her even if I can't find her. I need to disappear her in myself. This isn't my idea. None of the ideas are mine. If I don't slap my face right now, you may never hear from me again.

Notebook #6

Practice

Hi there. I'm going to give you some tips on feeling as confident as you look. Many people have a hard time with this; some of us seem to come off as more confident than we are. This may have to do with your childhood. It may have to do with the messages you get from the world, because we are all getting messages from the world all the time, often based on our appearance, on things we can't really control about ourselves.

And this is one of the first things that I want to talk about. You can control more than you think. You can control a lot about your appearance: I don't have to look like this, I don't have to wear this jacket, I don't have to do my hair like this. I have, at times in my life, walked out into the world in a way that makes me feel absolutely invisible. And on those days, I am invisible, most people don't see me. And there are other times where I don't want to be invisible, I want to be seen—and I want to be seen *as* a certain type of person in the world. And being seen that way is deeply important to me, on those days.

And I think that we aren't all given equal power, I think we all know that we aren't all equally *empowered* to learn the techniques for presenting, to the world, the self that we want to be seen as.

So, I know you came here for an acting class. And that's not exactly what we're going to be doing. But it's connected, in the sense that this is a class about how to force the world to reflect back to you the image you would like to see yourself as, and to thereby project back to the world. So it's a kind of infinite loop, actually, where you're creating, in your mind, the best self for you. And you are visualizing that self. You can take your notebook and draw a sketch, you know, what you would look like, and what your clothing would be, and maybe even where you would be, like—maybe it's a café in Paris. So, you would take a picture, or draw a picture of yourself at a café in Paris. Maybe you would have a cigarette. Maybe you would be entertaining, you know, *passersby*, who are all turning their heads to look at you because you're so magnetic and so beautiful.

So, you have to fantasize a little bit first. And then? You have to go out and *get* it. And that's what we're going to learn how to do.

After the visualization stage, the next thing to do is to *experiment*, and that means to find a place that you feel safe: a place that you feel isn't going to reject you. So let's say you want to be a supermodel, but you're five foot four, and you are aware that most supermodels are not five foot four. So you might not want to actually go to a place that's full of supermodels. That might mean you want to avoid all of London, all of Paris, and all of New York, for instance.

Or, you know, *neighborhoods*. There are certainly neighborhoods in New York where everyone is not a supermodel, but you want to avoid the neighborhoods where they are, because you're setting yourself up for failure in that kind of situation. You are *self-sabotaging*.

And really, that's what this whole thing is an attempt to do. It is an attempt to forbid ourselves—*forbid* ourselves from self-sabotaging. Think about that for a minute. What is it to *sabotage the self*?

First of all, if you think about sabotage, the way I understand the word—and maybe I have it a little bit wrong—but the way I understand the word, it's like sinking somebody else's ship, right? It's like going underground or under the water in a scuba outfit, and drilling a hole in the hull of somebody else's ship, so that their ship goes down, and they sink, and they die.

What does it mean to do that to yourself? You are your own ship. Well, you're either on your own ship or you are your own ship, depending on how you think of the mind and the body, but anyway.

So how do you *become* this saboteur? How do you even *do* that? How do you drill a hole in your own guts so that everything spills out, and then you die? Well, I think if you're here, watching me, you know how you do that, because you're doing it to yourself *all the time*. And that's why you are looking for advice. For techniques, for *help*.

So what we're going to do is we're going to go find all those guts that have been spilling out everywhere we go. Because we've been drilling a hole in ourselves our whole lives. Our whole lives we've just been, just letting it all spill out—and, you know, not even go anywhere, it's not like we're giving it to somebody else, it's not like somebody else is getting to benefit from all that good stuff that's within us that we are constantly just letting come out. You know, it's just—a waste.

So? We're going to go find it. We're going to *gather* it from all the places where we let it spill—all the relationships, all the institutions. All of the moments, alone, where we've wanted to die. Where we've almost died. You know, because we've let so much of our life force out that there's almost nothing left inside. You know, these moments—you could probably make a list of them, it would probably be a very, very long list.

And we're going to go and visit each of those moments.

And we're going to gather, to gather all of that life force, all of that goodness, all of that complexity, all of that uniqueness.

And we're going to bring it back in, we're going to bring it back in.

It's as if the ship that's on the bottom of the ocean rises, comes to the surface, and emerges. And to the people watching who think it's a lost cause, who think that ship's gone—well, it's a miracle.

We're here to create *from* ourselves, *for* ourselves—and, therefore, for the world—a personal, personal miracle.

OKAY. IT'S OKAY.

I'm okay.

It's only a story. Eighty-three critics saw through it when it came out. It's a story and I fell for it. No victims. I'm okay. I love life. I'll kill her and then I can live. By killing her, I'll make us both complete.

And I don't even need to look for her. She'll come running, now that she knows. She'll come and I just have to wait.

This is it, the muscle building. My bright coherence starting to emerge.

CELIA CAME BY with food this morning: a dozen eggs, a box of cereal, milk. Two packs of cheese, some cans of tuna and sardines. We sat at the Formica table and drank tea from the garden. Rosemary, which stimulates the brain.

Celia didn't look good. Her hair was so bright, like a streetlight. It fell too far down her back. Not right. And so smooth. But we had a nice conversation. She let me talk about Tala without interruption, and even suggested a new place I might find her, writing an address on the back of my hand. I told Celia about the office in the alley and I showed her the cards. As we sat together, the earth was mostly quiet, still, but the one time it shook and I fell to the ground, Celia picked me up and settled me back in my chair without a word.

She looked at the cards, turned them over in her hands.

"I can see how these might compel you," she said. She was still being nice. So different from when we talked at the bar. *Night and day.*

"What do you mean, compel me?" I asked.

"I mean that these are the kinds of things that you think about. You have always been drawn to think about these things. You're always talking about panic and anxiety. I never knew what you meant since you've always seemed so calm and together."

She was turning the cards over, one by one, then stacking them on the table between us. After she'd read each side of each card out loud, she straightened the small stack and centered them on the tabletop. GET IT / LOSE IT was on top.

"I have to go," Celia said. Her eyes were clouded, unfocused, but she was smiling as she said it. "Go to that address. It will help you find Tala."

I watched her walk across the patio, which at that moment was violently undulating. Celia moved straight through it, steady as she goes. *She walks on water.*

The address turned out to be just a few blocks from the office in the alley, and also just a few blocks from the bar. Center City is not that big, actually. The city itself is big—the Greater City—it's so big it can't be fathomed, you can't *get your head around it.* (More junk. Why would I want that.)

Get it into your head, they used to yell. Who did? Were they yelling? Some things sound like yelling even if they aren't. Get it through your fucking head. Implied.

I can't get it out of my mind. Can't get you out of my mind. Maybe all I need is to get her out of my mind.

But I was talking about Center City. It's not big. You can walk it. At least you can walk it when the ground lets you. I'm right in the middle of it, in its midst. Wide street, shops. Parked cars, a figure here and there. Big sliding glass doors. Yellow beige silver black. Bright. Some numbers. I compare them to what's written on my hand.

There's a sign above the doors but I can't read it. Glaring in the sun. I'm standing in front of the door. There are pieces of paper, flyers, taped to the inside of the thick glass. One says "KNIT'N'STITCH—All Levels." One says "FIND YOUR AUTHENTIC VOICE— Everyone Can Sing!"

I walk closer and the doors slide open on their own.

THIS OFFICE IS not like the other office, the one I viewed through the one-way-mirrored windows. The other office was calm, the figures inside were occupied, some alone and some with one another, but they were not flinging themselves this way and that, toward and away from each other, or circling like vultures closing in on a tiny mouse.

This office, behind the automatically opening un-mirrored glass doors, is only vultures, and entering it is like entering the field below the vultures, or the sky among the vultures, and as I walk across the threshold of the wide un-mirrored glass doors I become smaller with every jagged step (because the field is moving, or the sky is moving), and as the vultures approach and begin to circle around me, opening and closing their beaks and making screeching sounds at me and then over me at each other, and as they hold their claws out in front of me, their claws dripping with papers and pens and hard brown or clear boards with metal clips at the top, I close my eyes and try to still myself and balance like the Breton sailor, and only then can the voice in my silent mouth speak, only then can I hear the voice in my mouth, which is saying, softly and then increasing in volume and force: *Turn back, turn back, get out and then get what you got.*

It is so good to receive instruction. It is so good to understand.

I spin around and the vultures follow me and one of them shoves a piece of paper in my hand and the un-mirrored glass doors open automatically and I walk through them and take ten steps to the left and fall to the ground and then when the ground calms down I stand back up.

IN THE DREAMS, sometimes I am restrained. Sometimes I am pummeled and sometimes I am on a stage. Sometimes I am in a closet receiving instructions through the door. Sometimes I am penetrated and sometimes I am made to penetrate. Sometimes I am bound by ropes or cloth, suspended. Sometimes I am submerged in water. Sometimes I am left naked in the cold.

It's strange that I'm having these dreams and it's strange that I'm enjoying them since I have not had sex in many years and I had not enjoyed having sex for many years before that. I used to masturbate regularly but I can't remember the last time I masturbated. Though yesterday I woke up from one of the dreams having ejaculated all over Tala's bed, a watery spray that I couldn't control, a substance I struggled to recognize as mine.

As I walk away from the second office, from its vultures and their claws, I am thinking about the dreams and about how Tala is both in and not in them. Not pictured in them but still somehow there. Once I'm upright again I don't find it hard to walk, the ground has softened, I am not even using my cane. I try to count the dreams and determine their sequence, their pattern. And then I'm in the curved alley and in front of the other office, the first one, with its dark mirrored doors.

THERE ARE PEOPLE inside. The same people or different people, similarly dressed from the cheap side of the mall.

As before, some of them are sitting in the cubicles around the room's perimeter. Some of them are on the phone. Two of them, as before, are more in the middle of the room, talking, but this time instead of standing they are on high stools, each of them on one stool, with a third stool between them, and sitting on the third stool is a rectangular metal object. One of the people sitting on one of the stools is holding a metal cylinder that appears to be attached to the object on the stool, though whatever it is that attaches it, wires I guess, is hard to make out from a distance through the mirrored glass.

The person holding the cylinder is wearing an expression of distress, which is somehow easy to make out. I mean that the emotion of the person's expression is clear, while other aspects of the person are blurry. It's as if the emotion of the person is in the center of a photograph taken with a camera that has had Vaseline smeared on the edges of its lens. Not only has the rest of the person on the stool become blurry, but the entire scene behind the windows has become blurry, while the clear emotion, *distress*, has become clearer and more all-encompassing.

I can feel the emotion's clarity extend toward the windows, the only thing that separates me from the scene inside, and while there is something compelling about the prospect of receiving it, of welcoming it and letting it and its clarity overtake me, I am aware of my prior agenda, and my awareness of my prior agenda makes me take a step back, and then two steps back, away from the window and back toward my little bungalow, toward my project, toward my notebooks and the priorities listed on the cabinet door of the kitchenette, neglected now for many days.

I take two more steps back and the scene is erased as the windows become opaque, reflecting only the sun.

The way home is calm. A soft layer of sand beneath my feet, a soft wind breathing on the sand. My left hand is in my pocket. My right hand is still holding the piece of paper I was handed. It has words on it. Everyone Can Sing!

> *this one here goes there*
> *this one there stays there, asymmetry*

asymmetry goes the round the round
I have not yet traveled to the land of return
I have not yet traveled and cannot return
sun out there, sun in here
part your life in the middle / it fails / falls

VII.

VOICE (Notebook #7)

CORE
Every voice has a core. You can sing through it, or over it or around it. The core of every voice is in its Ah.

SUBTRACTION
Essence of voice is subtractive. Excess covers the core, disguises

it. To sing through the excess is to strain, is futile. A future sculpture singing through the marble block.

HUM
Humming is a tool. When the core is weak, hum to find it. Hum all the time. Do not mind the stares.

FOR THE FIRST decade of my professional career, I was encouraged to keep my voice high—to preserve my girlish register—to take advantage of the brute currency allotted to a young actress who can play even younger than she is, in role after role (roles that invariably equated coming-of-age with seducing or being seduced by a much older man).

I would say my line and the director, or the assistant director, usually a man but not always a man, would say, "Perfect. Now can we go again but with a bit more vulnerability? Let her be fragile, let her essential fragility show."

And I would do it again, pulling the back of my tongue up against my tonsils, just a little bit, shrugging my shoulders forward just a little bit, curling my lips into the tiniest, impish smile—just a little—performing this sequence of micro-movements that I had semiconsciously discovered would result in the shift of pitch that was being requested of me, from a D-flat to an E, an F, or even a G.

Had I been more business-minded, I could have taught a course, I could have founded an academy or written a book, or at least a pamphlet or a brochure. It would be titled *How to Play Thirteen at Eighteen, and Sixteen at Twenty-Two, and Accept the Most Lucrative Tongues Down Your Lucrative Throat!*

But I was not business-minded. I was fickle and coarse and unwise, "bratty," "spoiled," and "rebellious"—once, I spat the lucrative tongue back into a Golden Globe nominee's throat and caused a scandal on set, though the PA who walked me back to the trailer, a woman old enough to be my mother, said, "Well done, girl," and gave my shoulder a squeeze. (That the Golden Globe nominee—the only tongue in my history of forced tongues connected to a famous name—happened to die tragically in a boating accident soon after the production wrapped, and that he had in any case been young and hapless, not in the business long enough to have left a legacy of complaints, meant that even had I decided to *go public* with my revelation, when added to everyone else's concurrent revelations, at a moment that collected revelations, it would have been swallowed by the rest.)

I was not the star, back then, never the star. I was "supporting." I was support. The trailer, if there was a trailer, was always shared.

SINGLE

Voice is not single. The core is not single. Language fails to provide for the complexity of the core. If this failure is not made to be a virtue it will become a flaw.

FOR THE SECOND decade of my career, after I was no longer able to time travel, when playing under eighteen was a line struck from my résumé (was the incident with the Golden Globe nominee a factor too? who's to say) we were encouraged to lower our voices, to seek a womanly, sensuous gravel, a smoker's husk.

Then, when I moved firmly to stage work and was called upon to *project*, I learned from a speech pathologist that I would lose my voice completely if I didn't stop lowering it. This woman, who was ancient already, whose hair was a beehive, who wrote poems on a typewriter in her spare time, assigned me three months' worth of daily exercises. The goal was to find, and then strengthen, my so-called *authentic* voice.

I liked the speech pathologist's exercises. I would do them high and I would do them low. I didn't want to know my authentic voice, I wanted to know my range.

It_is_only_eleven_o'clock
All_our_array_is_ancient
Eddie_is_outdoors
It_attains_an_end_in_itself

I_urge_all_on_in_eager_endeavors
It_is_emphasized_in_earnest
Iceland_oozes_ice_and_icebergs

What is the thing that's true about five hundred people singing the same song when most of them are off-key. How in the ears of the listener, the wrong notes cancel each other out.

running and punning and gunning
spinning and grinning and winning
singing and flinging and swinging
tabbing and crabbing and grabbing
cracking and clacking and tracking

SHADOW

The core does not have a shadow
but the voice has shadows. Shadow
can be before, below, or behind,
or in more than one place at a
time. When people hear voice,
shadow is what they hear.

gliding and sliding and hiding
raiding and blockading and masquerading
jagging and flagging and tagging
sailing and hailing and trailing
gaming and aiming and acclaiming
painting and plainting and chanting
blaring and snaring and tearing
celebrating and elating and anticipating
separating and narrating and translating
shaking and breaking and quaking.

The theater of war is the whole arena, the whole field. The outdoor stage where my disaster happened. My catastrophe. My change. Breaking and quaking. Who or what is a bad actor?

Or how, once the anesthetic begins to work, all you can see from the gurney is the eyes of a man (it was always a man) peering at you over a blue-and-white mask—hair in a net, or no hair, no matter—everything covered (as in all masquerades) except the eyes.

Like an executioner's hood, maybe.

Life, death, the right to remain unknown, unrecognized.

Veiled, masked, to not be surveilled.

And/or/also. The exhibitionist's theater, the exhibitionist's mask, the bottom.

— To speak the voice's shadows —
To hollow out the core — The shadows play backward and forward at
the same time — Do shadows leave
traces? Impressions? — How do you
know when a metaphor is junk —
How old is it — How long has it
been in your body — Who put it
there —

WHEN I OFFERED to teach voice to Tala, it seemed like an obvious suggestion. She had just moved in, she was bored with her job, she would hum around the house. Nina Simone. Joni Mitchell. Old stuff, which surprised me, since she was young.

She was noncommittal. We were sitting at the Formica table, drinking water with lemon. She confessed she had always been self-conscious about her singing. I told her one day she'd learn that there is no self of which to be conscious. She gave me a look, then threw her head back and laughed. That was the last we talked of it.

I am beginning to forget what she looks like. I can picture the gestures, I can feel her mass, the outline of her figure. Like a ghost in the shadows, like an *impression*. I can see her dark hair falling down her back, or tied in two compact buns beneath her ears. I can see her slim fingers handling one or another of my chipped porcelain cups. But I am having increasing trouble resolving an image of her face.

Today has been difficult. Forms arrived in the mail that I need to fill out and return if I wanted to continue to receive *relief*. The forms confuse me. It is implied that if

I answer the questions wrong, the relief might be canceled. If the relief is canceled, I don't know what I'll do. But how is it possible that everyone who needs relief also knows how to fill out the forms? It's not; it's not possible that everyone who needs it is receiving relief.

Celia will help me. I have Celia, I am fortunate. Does everyone have a Celia? It's such an accident that I do. A fortunate accident. Unlike the unfortunate accidents.

The card that arrived this morning said on one side STAY IN YOUR OWN BUSINESS. On the other it said LOVE WHAT IS. What is = my accident, my Celia, my relief. What's my business?

I have lost my way. The words swim in the air.

YOUR . . . OWN . . . LOVE.

The cards are now taped up on the pantry door, all of them together, jumbled and overlapping, where my chalk lists used to live.

RESOLVE, AS YOURSELF, YOUR
DISCORDANCE WITH REALITY.

CROSS THE THRESHOLD OF THE
VISIBLE WORLD.

Together, overlapping, they have covered my plan. They have smothered my project.

LAST NIGHT I was woken by a voice out the bedroom window. A sharp light darting around, tracing chaotic patterns on the wall. The voice was a harsh whisper, loud and unidentifiable. "Tala! Tala!" the voice said. "Tala! Are you there? Tala!"

I put the pillow around my ears and hummed. I watched the light dart around the room, then exit through the window behind my head. When the sun woke me up, I was still clutching the pillow. I opened my mouth and reproduced the sounds I'd heard. It was easy, because it's easy to imitate a whisper. There is no timbre, no core, just technique. No, just shadow.

"Tala! Tala!"

I'm unbearably sad. I don't know if it's the forms and the precarity they represent, or the thought about fortunate accidents, or the whispered voice from last night, the near miss.

The sadness is familiar. I have described it in my notebooks in various ways.

Today I wrote, "like a hot white fire that starts inside and burns outward, turning everything into itself." The voice in my silent mouth recites distant lessons. How fire is power and light is truth.

Inner light, inner fire. Lessons that hide their weapons.

Lessons that don't admit their goal. Lessons that obliterate other, quieter lessons. Lesson upon obliterating lesson, building a case in favor of the core.

Which means, by necessity, a case against the shadows.

The first exercise is about hair.

Hair is really the first thing that people notice when they see us. And that goes for people who have no hair. Also, the absence of hair is the first thing people notice. So hair is really important.

My hair is just the way it is. I can't control it very much. I've tried to do all different things with it, and somehow it always ends up sort of the same. I don't really wash it, I don't style it. I never blow-dry it. Sometimes I dye it, just for fun—but it's just the way it is. So you know, do your thing with your hair, whatever your hair does for you. Let your hair do *that* thing. And that's the first lesson here.

The second lesson is: jackets. So. Next to the hair, the next thing people notice when you walk down the street—unless it's summer and you're not wearing a jacket, but let's just say it's not summer and you're wearing a jacket—the next thing people notice is your jacket. This is natural, because it's the largest item of clothing normally and it's covering a big part of your body, *and* it's covering the part of your body that is immediately below the hair. So after noticing the first thing, which is the hair, then it's just natural that it would be the jacket. So, you know, jackets signify— well, they signify various things. This one I'm wearing is kind of like a motorcycle jacket. It's not actually a motorcycle jacket. I mean, I wouldn't wear this on a motorcycle because it doesn't have the armor, you know, that you need if you ride a motorcycle to keep you from dying, if you fall, hopefully. But anyway, it's like a motorcycle-style jacket. So that signifies, I mean, it either signifies, Hey, I'm a motorcycle girl, I ride a motorcycle, or I grab the back of a motorcycle or, or maybe it just signifies I identify with a kind of tradition of, you know, riding free, right? Just hitting the road and going. And it has this sort of, you know, a sort of *feeling* to it.

And it's made of leather, this one is made of leather. You might be a vegan—you might be a vegan who doesn't mind wearing leather, in which case, you can totally wear a leather motorcycle jacket. But you also might be the kind of vegan who actually won't, actually won't really wear leather. And if that's who you are, they are making really kind of amazing fake leather motorcycle jackets now. I mean, they're really pretty incredible. So you have that option. You could be the third type of vegan, which is the type of vegan that will wear leather, but only if it's used, like only if the jacket itself, or the boots, or the belt, or whatever the leather thing is, was made in the past. And has been, sort of, on the planet for a while, and purchased at a used-clothing store or on eBay or Etsy or—well, so you feel like you're not actually killing an animal by wearing that jacket. So you know, whichever, whatever your thing is. Or maybe you're a carnivore, and you just like go into the leather store, and say like, Hey, you know, which is the freshest-killed jacket? So whoever you are, you just get the jacket that you want.

And you might not wear a motorcycle jacket at all, you might wear sort of like a camel hair coat. I mean, I have never really understood what a camel hair coat is. I think it's a color that they're talking about—is it made of camel? I don't know. But I think of it as that kind of preppy, soft, like as if you *brushed* it kind of a very *streamlined* coat. So you know, you could wear that. Or you could be sort of like a parka girl, you know, so.

Whatever it is, you've got your hair, you've got your coat, or a jacket. And, and that's kind of half your body that now is *cloaked* in the image that you are trying to project.

So I think maybe it's time to go out and try to—you have your drawing of who you want to be. You have your image of where you want to go to be that person. You have your hair, you have your coat—obviously put something on the bottom, put on some pants or a skirt or some shorts or whatever, that kind of goes with the hair, you know, and some shoes. Shoes are actually really important too. But you know, we're kind of working on *this* right now.

So we're going to take this pause, because it's really important to practice, you know, and that's really the last thing I'm going to say in this first lesson is how important it is to practice. *Practice* is a big word, I mean, PRACTICE. You know, you can practice piano, you can practice yoga, you can practice meditation, you can practice kindness—and you can practice being yourself in the world, but without insecurity, without self-annihilation, without self-hatred, without low self-esteem, which I guess is sort of a double negative. So, let's say *with* high self-esteem. You can practice being a better version of yourself. And the only way to do that? The only way to do that is the *opposite* of what everyone tells you. It is to look at the *outsides* of other people and *emulate them.*

But never exactly. Never. Exactly.

So for instance, I'm making this video after watching an entire online class from the actress Natalie P_____. And she's beautiful. And she's, she's gorgeous. And she seems very competent. And she, you know, is sharing all of the, all of the insights that she has from her long, long career. I mean, she's not very old, but you know, a long career because she started as a child acting in movies— and maybe theater, maybe television, I don't know. But anyway, uh, my first thought was, Oh, I want some of that. I want some of that confidence. I want some of that—like, how do you get to *be* like that? So I watched and I studied, and of course, the fact that she was talking about acting made the whole thing kind of like this wild mirror game, you know, like, I'm looking at her talking about acting, but I'm thinking about acting like her, like acting while talking about acting. And so there was this whole sort of, like, kind of meta backdrop for it all.

But ultimately, I really just wanted to see how close I could get to *being* Natalie P_____. A person I've never spent any time thinking about until now. So this is sort of a surprise. But that's one of the things about me, some-times things just kind of pop up. Anyway. I realized once I started to—once I turned the camera on and started, you know, I did my makeup and I tried to do my hair a little bit like her. But like I said, my hair is stubborn. It's just my hair. She wasn't in a motorcycle jacket. I don't have a lot of clothes here. I'm in a hotel. So.

And I realized, I can't actually be Natalie P_____. I'm always me—as she herself said, because she was talking in one of her les-sons about playing Jackie Kennedy and about playing, you know, *any* real person and she said, "You're always you." So you have to make a blend, you have to make a, like an *average* between the person you're trying to be, and you. And I think this is also applicable to the practice of going out in the world as the person you want to be, which can only ever be some kind of average or combination or . . . *melding* of other people. You see their outsides because you can't see their insides. Their outsides and your insides, who you are, and what you see, what you hear—because this also applies to how you speak—blended together into the best *you*, because there's nothing else you can work with. The shit in here you're stuck with. The most beautiful, desirable things out *there* are the best you can get.

So go get them. Mix them up with the shit in here. And then trust that you're going to fool not just everyone you encounter, but ultimately—with practice—yourself.

Thank you so much for being here for this first lesson. Now, go out there. Go be you.

I VAGUELY REMEMBER watching the video, though I don't remember how I came across it. I vaguely remember transcribing the lesson by hand. I vaguely remember improvising my transcription in front of the camera, re-performing the lesson alone, for no one. I vaguely remember uploading the new video of my improvisation to a transcription service, then correcting it and printing it out, and cutting the pages to fit inside a slim, tall notebook with a green cover. I vaguely remember writing a title on the notebook's cover: #6. Practice.

fire . . . under . . . breath
breath . . . under . . . arc
arc fast . . . under . . . stand
stand fast . . . arc . . . away
if you can learn to breathe like this
you can say anything
to anyone

VIII.

I RETURNED TO the orange notebook—Phantasy—
and to the scenarios listed there. I was seated at the Formica table and looking out toward the patio, which was
convulsing violently, ceaselessly, after these last weeks
of relative calm. The fractured concrete rose and fell in
waves, undulating like the cracked leather skin of some
great alien ready to give birth. I am a parasite on that
alien, I thought, a freeloader. No wonder I can't take responsibility enough even to picture this act that I claim
is so necessary, so urgent. No wonder the best I can do

is to picture practicing the act, its rehearsal. Not the act itself.

I am not a physically violent person. I have never struck a soul, except onstage of course. And, twice, in self-defense. If I could kill Tala without blood, without pain—if I could somehow cast a spell to rearrange her molecules and release her to a different plane, a different realm, a better one—I would. *In a heartbeat*, as they say. In a heartbeat I would spare us both, without pain and without a second thought.

But there is always a second thought. And there is always pain. Right now, and ever since she appeared in my life, Tala has been the site of both. The bottomless self-doubt, the push and pull of desire (it was when she left that my need to kill her intensified; when she was here, I deflected, deferred)—and the pain, so hard to characterize, but impossible to ignore.

The notebooks—seven in all—have collected themselves into an unruly but still movable stack. I carry them with me wherever I go. They are my interlocutors; they hold the membrane in place.

Before Coach X, there had been other coaches; before the gentle professor, there had been other professors, gentle and not. Other phrases. Junk and not. I don't know, I can't know, where they entered my body and what they did once they arrived. Maybe they bred, and like the alien concrete baby trying to emerge from the patio, they're readying to come out. They want to live.

How important it is to practice! I have been practicing walking around the bungalow. I have become bolder, stronger. There are actions that feel impossible before you've made them—balancing positions, or simple flexes of an underused muscle—that only require a bit of determination to accomplish. A bit of belief. To go from stillness, from "I can't!" to movement—"I did!" This is how I have improved my ability to walk on the shaking ground.

It has also helped to sing while I practice. My footfall is heavy, ugly, asymmetrical, as I stomp and stagger around the living room, choosing to test my progress when the undulations are at their most extreme. But when I sing at the same time, whether it's a low steady drone or a repeated high arpeggio or a familiar melody, the heavy ugly footfalls become interesting. They require the voice as a counterpart, they need an other to play against. And though the voice, ethereal and irrevocably mortal, appears as an overlay, it's not: if it disappears the whole thing falls apart.

If I forget to sing as I walk, I fall. When this happens it's proof that the shadow, accustomed to being secondary, has risen in value. In relative power. That the shadow is no more subordinate to the light.

J.P. says *revolution* and I don't know what he means. But right now, for this instant, some kind of knowledge flashes through me. The flash makes me hold my breath, which makes me stop singing. The stopping singing again causes me to fall.

The flash is not the same thing as understanding. The flash is what understanding was invented to replace.

You SEE HOW I have detoured from the question about picturing my kill, how I avoid it with such skill? Actors move toward difficulty, toward intensity. But a moving toward can simultaneously be a moving away. (Theorists do this too; the gentle professor did.) I wrote in On Being a Student, "What if the most difficult question to face is not 'What would it mean to actually kill Tala?' or 'What would it mean to let her live?' but rather, 'What if I'm asking a question that isn't mine?'"

I gather my thoughts. I gather myself. I pull myself up off the floor, stagger over to the daybed. There's a knock on the door. Of course. I hope it's J.P., so I can tell him about the flash. "Come in!" I call. "I'm here!"

It isn't J.P.

The door opens, and bright light haloes the head of the visitor, so all I can see is a human figure in silhouette. I recognize Tala—tall, long hair, ankle boots—and then the door closes and the light is cut off and in the shadow I see standing before me the bartender, the first one, the one who reminded me of Tala but is actually somebody else. The bartender is holding out a white card with black writing on it. "I found this outside your door. Can I come in?"

THE BARTENDER IS wearing a backpack, which she takes off and drops on the kitchen table. She unzips it and starts to remove its contents: a bag of small oranges, a tin of coffee, toothpaste, a notebook and some pens, a bag of chocolate malt balls. "Care package," she says. "Can I sit?"

The bartender talks for a while, though it's hard to say what she's talking about. At one point she holds up the card that she'd found on the stoop and rips it up. At another point, she asks me a question over and over again, and even grabs my shoulders and gives them a shake when I can't figure out the right answer. At another point she repeats Tala's name, over and over, her face inches from mine. Her pores are visible, open. She seems to be sweating from effort.

"Tala," she says. "Tala, Tala, Tala."

I DON'T REMEMBER the bartender's departure. I found myself on the daybed as the sun flared briefly behind some distant building, then disappeared beneath it. The fruit and toothpaste, notebook, and the rest of the bartender's care package lay in a haphazard pile on the kitchen table.

Tala is crawling toward me. I can't tell where she is, how far away, how long it will take. She is a shadow, a beautiful deep shadow humming with life. The surface she is crawling on undulates like the surface of the ocean, or like the patio when it appears as an alien's pregnant body, or like the street outside when I go out to look for her. The undulating surface is also a shadow, a shadow made of many other shadows. The surface, though it isn't smooth or easy, is supporting Tala, it will not let her fall. Her crawl is complicated, each pull forward seems to require a different set of movements. Her body is engaged, no part of it is passive, no movement is the same as any other.

She is not speaking but she is trying to tell me something. What is she trying to tell me? I wonder if I can learn to crawl from Tala, the way I learned to stand from the Breton sailor, the way I learned to concentrate all of my energy into my core. To watch Tala crawl is to watch a body that has no core, or a body that is all core, no *extremities*. It is to wonder, in a flash (which doesn't feel like understanding, but which takes understanding's place), if the question—the one seeded in me by the acting coach, the gentle professor, the Breton sailor, and so many others—has been wrong all along.

And then to wonder if even this is too simple, too brute.

How do you answer a question that might be half right and half wrong? Half yours and half not, or half yours by right or by choice, and half yours by accident or fortune, by coercion, or by force?

What if there are more than two halves?

How do you not confuse being wronged with being right?

What if there is nothing but shades of wrong? What if those shades are beautiful, forgiving, supportive, like the surface Tala is crawling on, toward me. Feeling me as she crawls. Seeing me.

I don't think I am voicing this, I don't think I am voicing anything. But Tala responds, through the tunnel of distance, the over-thereness of her approach. "I love you," she says, and her voice travels as if it's traveling through an ocean, full of threatened but ongoing life. "Come back," she says. "I'll meet you halfway," she says.

"You are working hard," she says. "But you are still *working*. Who are you working for?"

"I love you," she says. "I love you, and I will die for you, because you have already died for me. We die for each other, can't you see? We offer to die because we want to live. I love you. Breathe.

"Remember what we learned when we were learning how to sing? When you breathe with everything you have, you can say anything to anyone. You can say it to yourself."

THAT WAS YESTERDAY. This morning I ate an orange, put away the rest of the bartender's gifts, and gathered up the black-and-white cards, un-taping the ones I'd posted on the chalkboard-painted cabinet door. The tape left remnants, sticky rectangles on the black ground. I cleaned the door gently, with a sponge dipped in dish soap, clearing the last bits of chalk and adhesive. The surface began to dry in patches, a mottled pattern of darker and lighter black.

I arrayed the cards on the floor in a neat grid. Because they were double-sided, I couldn't look at all of the language at once. I arranged and rearranged the cards, flipped one over, then another, then flipped them back. I got my kitchen scissors from the cutlery drawer and separated words that needed to be separate. The cards fragmented into smaller cards, irregularly shaped.

What relief, to cut the cards and liberate the words from each other! What relief, to rearrange their meaning! If only I could find Tala, and tell her how it feels!

who would be wrong
dizziness   freedom

experience makes experience
love   stay   language
authentic is arbitrary   consensus
your   own   love
get   set

IX.

THE NEW LIST: things to kill instead of Tala.

1. Junk phrases
2. Purity
3. Equation: clarity = light
4. Equation: centrality = singularity
5. Fear of the dark
6. Fear of exposure
7. Fear of

Notes:

The ground still undulates, but I don't always feel it.

Cognitive dissonance points to a faulty expectation.

Assonance is for asses.

Resonance travels through substance, like Tala crawling toward me (in a vacuum, there is no sound).

Is this true, or does it only *feel* true?

I HAD PASTED the cut-up words from the various cards into the inside of a manilla file folder, so that the folder looked clean and blank from the outside and the reassembled language—a poem, I thought—would appear like a secret code when it was opened.

Walking to deliver it, I noticed there was less sand on the ground, less wind, than I'd grown used to. The ground was still, mostly. I fell, but only once. I picked myself up and moved on.

I hummed while I walked, as I have been reminding myself to do. When I teach voice, I hold my hands up to my chin, horizontal, tips touching, to form a stage to support the sound.

When I act as someone else, I am unashamed. When I walk down the street, humming softly to prevent myself from falling, I am full of self-consciousness. Figures walk past. Can they hear me hum? What does it mean if they can? What would it mean if they can't?

Walking to deliver the cut-up poem, humming, I did not feel alone. I felt Tala's presence, a distant presence, a slow approach. I felt Tala's love, but as if distorted through a film. The movie plays in slow motion. It is difficult to hum without humming a familiar tune.

WHEN I ARRIVED at the office in the alley in Center City, nothing was as I'd expected it to be. The windows were dark, the fluorescent lights were off. One of the windows had been smashed in, cracks radiating out from a central hole, prevented from shattering completely by layers of cardboard and crisscrossed clear packing tape. Words had been written on the mess with white spray paint, but I couldn't read the words. I couldn't read the situation. I stood and looked, from across the alley, with the manilla-folder poem in my hand. Even the voice in my silent mouth had nothing to say.

There was a figure standing between me and the windows. Standing, head down, as still as a statue. We stood like that, separated by the width of the alley and by our different vantage points—I could see the figure, but the figure couldn't see me—for a while, possibly a long while. Then I crossed the street and tapped the figure on the shoulder.

It was a person my age or older, small framed, wearing a knit cap, a saggy beige jacket, overalls, and a deflated expression. A can of spray paint lay sideways on the ground at the person's feet.

I introduced myself, held out my hand.

"I'm Trix," a voice said, breathy and low. "Do you know what happened?"

I shook my head. "I came to deliver something." I held up the manilla file folder and watched Trix's eyes take it in.

"Me too," Trix said, and smiled. "And I'm pissed that they're not here to receive it."

WE SAT AT the bar and ordered beers, and I listened to Trix's story. It was five o'clock and people were starting to stream in. Trix and I leaned toward each other to drown out the noise.

"I'm a timid person by nature," Trix began, "or by nurture, could be, don't know. That's probably how I ended up here anyway." The story took a long time to tell. We ordered two rounds from the bartender, who had greeted me upon entering with a smile and a "It's good to see you!" that struck me as overly emphatic. It was the bartender who looked like Tala, though for some reason today the resemblance seemed only superficial. "You too!" I replied, trying to mirror the emphatic quality of the bartender's voice. Neither of us mentioned yesterday's visit, the care package, the way she'd shaken my shoulders and held my face in her hands.

"When you have made up a story in your head as a way of connecting observations or experiences that don't easily add up, you can get attached to the story in a way that is similar to the way you can get attached to the story of an experience that you had but that did not make sense because you weren't given all of the information necessary to make sense of it at the time" (this was how Trix's narration began). "It's like what happens to children who experience violent childhood events and have to fill in the parts of the story that the adults, whether by malice, ineptitude, or fear, or out of a well-meaning sense of protectiveness, didn't share."

Trix went on to tell me what had brought them to the office in the curved alley, how they had been handed a brochure just as I had, but months before me, by an acquaintance, and how they had responded to a follow-up mailing by enrolling in a course that promised to help participants *lose* their faulty expectations, let go of disappointments, and *get on with their lives.* They described an intricate set of rhetorical exercises that the people in the office led, exercises that seemed designed—in retrospect—to scramble people's ability to think for themselves, while claiming that *learning to think for oneself* was the whole point. The exercises included some of the phrases that were printed on my stack of cards: "Get what you got"; "Stay in your business"; "Love what is"; "Who would be wrong if your life began to work?"

I asked about what I'd seen through the mirrored window, the cans and strings, the emotional scenes, the hugs. Trix said the only way to tell me what went on behind those windows was to demonstrate for me. (*On me* is what they actually said.) They asked the bartender for two glasses of water, then removed the cord from their hoodie and tied one end of it around each glass, draping a napkin folded into a rectangle across the center of the cord. They put their hand on one glass and had me hold the other. Then, in a low, concentrated voice, they asked me a series of questions. The pace of the questions sped up steadily and the tone intensified as I responded; Trix leaned in closer after each response.

I can't tell you what the questions were, or what my answers were. Both vanished instantly into the air. What I mean is that the meaning of the words vanished beneath the logic of their manipulation. That the part of my brain that was trying to keep up with the logic of the interaction was overloaded, making the part of my brain that might be able to discern any flaws in that logic, or any misleading repurposing of my words, quiet. What I mean is that, like the time Coach X talked Veronica out of her headache, my body and mind, my emotions and my spirit, everything that I had ever learned to call my self, was for the duration of the exercise converted into a stage upon which Trix was mounting their own performance. The performance was of an intensity that could only be felt by us two, I was a stage with a force field around me, and time sped back and forth along the string connecting the glasses we each clutched, back and forth without direction, scrambling the order of cause and effect.

At some point I lost track of who was asking questions and who was answering them, of who was leading and who was being led. This was a form of engagement with rules, and I had been taught the rules by enacting the form, like the improv game of "Yes, and" or like a magician's best trick. When it was over, I felt clear and empty and almost superhuman, the way you feel after vomiting when you are finally sure all the poison's been expelled. That blank-slate feeling, euphoric, when you get to *begin again*.

AFTER THE EUPHORIA came a sharp pain in my right hand, a violent sting or burn. I thought of my notebooks. I thought, *This pain is the feeling of the words I need to write.*

I looked at Trix, I'm sure my eyes were swamped with gratitude if not tears, I looked at Trix and smiled slightly and whispered, "Thank you, thank you," and then Trix, who was not smiling, lifted a hand and slapped me across the face.

TRIX HELD MY wrist and pulled the glass shards from my palm while the bartender cleared the rest of the shattered glass from the bar. The sweatshirt cord was coiled on the bar like a snake; the folded napkin that had lain neatly on top of it had blown away. Trix looked up from my palm, eyes gentle.

"I'm sorry," they said. "I had to show you. Now you know."

I DID NOT know, or I couldn't be sure that I knew. But I felt the film begin to reverse, the tears of gratitude in my eyes become reabsorbed, the pain in my hand begin to lift, and I felt the force field that had surrounded the two of us begin to erode, letting others, the bar, the bartender, the world, in. The audio mix in the room shifted. As the voice next to me, Trix's voice, fell silent, all the other voices in the room flared. We had been alone in conversation, but we were not alone. We were alone and not alone, both things true at the same time.

I looked at Trix while also looking over their shoulder at the room. The voice in my silent mouth was asking, *Can we live with this? Can we live with all of this? Can we live?*

On impulse, I began to interpret the voice for Trix. On impulse I repeated, word for word, what the voice had asked. But at the moment I spoke Trix was glancing at their phone, and at the same moment the person behind us burst into laughter at some unknown prompt, and Trix looked up and said, "Sorry?" and I smiled and said, "Nothing," and gently shook my head. After we paid the bartender, took our jackets from the hooks, and put them on, Trix and I stood up from our stools at the same time.

"Is the ground moving?" I asked.

Trix paused, then nodded.

"A little."

LATER THAT WEEK, my phone rang. I was crouched down on the patio, trimming the rosemary. I didn't pick up the phone, I waited for the message to be recorded, then forgot about it. The next morning drinking tea made from the rosemary I'd trimmed, I listened to the message.

It was one of the theater directors who had called me after I'd made my apology in the park, who had asked me if I wanted to be a part of her next play, and who had said, when I said no, that she understood, which confused me because I did not understand.

She was calling, she said, to invite me to the show's opening performance. It wasn't really a performance, she said, it was an *encounter*, and she and her collaborators would be honored if I might be an audience-participant. No pressure, she said, you can also just watch. We would be so happy to see you there.

The opening is this evening. I had written down the address on the chalkboard door in the kitchenette. Not really an address, a public square, on the far edge of Center City. It would be a substantial walk.

Daylight savings time started yesterday; the director

and her collaborators seem to have calibrated the performance time to coincide with the sunset hour. If the performance isn't too long, I'll be able to make the walk home before darkness falls.

IT IS STRANGE to prepare to leave the house and head for a destination where I am expected, where I may meet people who are interested in meeting me.

It is strange to get dressed, to lift one leg and then the other, to balance while putting on a pair of pants, and not to fall. It is strange to feel the ground shudder, briefly, and then become still. To know it will shudder again, and become still again.

It is strange, it is more than strange, to walk through a door to the outside, and to have realized that something was forgotten inside—a jacket, since it might get cool—and to return indoors to get the jacket and step back out, all in a fluid, connected set of motions. Am I acting?

A person leaves the house to walk to an early evening performance, realizes she's forgotten her jacket, returns to retrieve it. Locks the door behind her and pauses. The sun is low and bright, the sun is *in her face*. She squints, allows her eyes to adjust. Slings her jacket over her shoulder and crosses the small concrete patio to unlatch the gate.

To get to the public square where the performance will be taking place, I need to walk through Center City to its far edge. I walk at a comfortable pace on the sidewalk, which is covered with a thin layer of sand. There is no wind.

Cars stream by, steady in their flow. More cars that I had seen on my outings to the first office, to the other office, or to the bar. Where had the cars gone? Are they back to stay? Infrequently, I pass figures walking on the sidewalk, on the other side of the street and on my side of the street. I nod, and am ignored. I nod, and the nod is returned. These variations repeat—ignored, returned—as I proceed from block to block.

When I reach Center City, with the higher buildings and narrower streets and alleys, shadows begin to dominate my field of vision. Shadows falling on entire sides of buildings and sidewalks, shadows cast by buildings falling on other buildings. Shadows falling off figures and landing on the ground. My own shadow, which I know is behind me, though I don't turn to look.

The shadows are a comfort. I listen to the voice in my silent mouth, which quotes from the notebook called VOICE:

"The core does not have a shadow but the voice has shadows. Shadow can be before, below, or behind, or in more than one place at a time. When people hear voice, shadow is what they hear. — To speak the voice's shadows — *To hollow out the core* —"

The shadows are a comfort, a challenge, a comfort. Tala crawling toward me. Trix slapping my face. My bandaged hand burns.

Soon I'm walking past the office in the alley with the mirrored windows. The windows have been covered with plywood, the plywood covered with graffiti. The graffiti is not legible, but I stare at it anyway, take a picture of it with my phone. As I put the phone away I notice a text from J.P.: "I have something for you you're gonna fucking love!"

The ground jolts, my knees buckle.

A squirrel crosses paths with a rat.

The shadows dance.

Leaving the curved alley, past a stretch of straighter blocks, past the second office, closed for the day, its flyered window lit from behind—"Everyone Can Sing!"—

The windows in the buildings are lit and unlit.

Figures move in some of them.

Shadows move and stay still.

I think about participating in the performance, about whether and how.

Or will I watch—

Will I approach as a potential performer, or will I approach as a potential observer, and is there a difference, or will I approach as myself? (Go be you!)

I turn the last corner, bringing the public square into

view. In the distance: figures, many of them, gathered. A low din, a rumble. The ground shudders. My knees buckle. What is an encounter made of? My shadow has moved in relation to my body. All the shadows have moved in relation. Are made of what. *Snap out of it*, the silent voice says. *If you snap out of it, you will be able.*

Say anything to anyone.

Snap back. Snap into it. Snap to.

It's strange how much I anticipate the approach to the square. How much I anticipate the moment when I am no longer approaching the square, the moment after I have arrived and am in the square, among the figures who have assembled there. Moving in relation; other footfalls, an other's breath. My shadow among their shadows, my shadow overlapping theirs.

I am almost close enough to make out individuals among the assembled figures. Almost close enough to try to distinguish the theater director from among the others, and to see what other familiar figures I might be able to single out.

I am close enough. A low hum emanates from the square. I crawl toward it on my own two feet.

Acknowledgments

For years, I've been telling people I'm writing about the intersection of self-help and self-actualization trainings with Method acting trainings, with an emphasis on what I see as shared (mis)uses of "authenticity" tropes and of the reperformance of trauma. Is this that book? Not exactly, and I'm not ready to stop having those conversations. If the length of these acknowledgments seems extreme for a short novel, it's partly because I can't tell what if any of my "research" ended up in this book, and yet this book was still somehow *all about* that research. Also, I love the deeply imperfect but—I find—meaningful task of recalling the gifts of others.

Thank you to everyone at Soft Skull—Mensah Demary, Cecilia Flores, tracy danes, Crystal Erickson, Lena Moses-Schmitt, Rachel Fershleiser, Kira Weiner, and all the workers who keep the press running. Thank you to Akin Akinwumi for believing this book would find a home, and for finding it. Thank you to Deborah Stratman for the films (including *For the Time Being*, which makes a cameo in these pages), for connection and conversations, and for being so amenable to lending a film still to the cover design.

In or around 2018, Bill Dietz very generously let me view the composition notebooks of Maryanne Amacher, an encounter I will never forget and which was elemental to this book: the phrase "Get out of the instrument a timbre (and continue to play, i.e., explore more specifically the collection of frequency characteristics within this timbre)" is Amacher's,* and the gesture of dividing a notebook practice into discrete topics for a time-bound process of setting down "what one knows" is inspired by her, but the composer in this book is fictional (as are all the characters), and I urge anyone who hasn't been exposed to Amacher's incomparable body of work to

---

* *Maryanne Amacher: Selected Writings and Interviews*, Amy Cimini and Bill Dietz, eds. Blank Forms, 2020.

seek it out: in the last few years, thanks to Dietz, Amy Cimini, and others, a trove of Amacher's written and di-agrammatical work, along with letters and interviews, is now available. Shonni Enelow's work on Method acting became a point of entry early on (Shonni's collabora-tion with David Levine, *A Discourse on Method*, makes a fictionalized cameo here), and I consumed Isaac But-ler's immersive *The Method* while revising. (Needless to say—junk phrase alert!—my narrator did not have the benefit of reading these books.) Brief but meaningful access to voice and acting lessons from my friends Sahra Motalebi and Serena Jost, and from the very gifted teacher Isaac Byrne (thanks, Leo Madriz, for the intro-duction) were instrumental, and served as both supple-ments and correctives for my experiences studying both arts in the last century. I would not have known of the remarkable Georgiana Peacher, whose vocal exercises from her 1966 book, *How to Improve Your Speaking Voice* (later repackaged for the 1980s as *Speak to Win*), are excerpted and adapted in these pages, if it weren't for Edwin Torres and his commitment to recirculating Peacher's poetry. It was a post of Anne Boyer's that led me to Hedwig Dohm's *Become Who You Are*, igniting my interest in Dohm and providing this book with an epigraph. Among the periodicals and podcasts in whose language and references I bathed for so many hours I can't know how to credit their influence, I'll highlight four, in part because they rely on the support of their audiences to survive: *Parapraxis* and its related podcast *Ordinary Unhappiness, Another Gaze: A Feminist Film Journal, Rendering Unconscious,* and *Why Theory?* I am grateful to the thinkers on the radical edge of contemporary psychoanalysis who have been cutting through so much bullshit in recent years, introducing liberating complexities to the concepts of trauma, (gender) identity, psychosis (Avgi Saketopoulou and Lara Sheehi, among others), and more, while breaking disciplinary tradition with their political will and activism for Palestinian life. I discovered the writings of Mari Ruti only after completing this book, but I feel the retroactive companionship of her thinking throughout; she died last year, while I was unknowingly waiting to meet her. My conversations with the late Lyn Hejinian about what it means for a poet to "have a novel" in them and my ongoing dialogue with my friend Renee Gladman about our attractions and resistances to the writing of fiction are never absent for long from my thinking or my notebooks, and were particularly present this time around. Jonathan Lethem, my first reader and most consistent interlocutor, was as always uncannily able to offer the right help at the right moments, and it was in his stacks that I found Anna Kavan's *Ice*, a novel that led directly, if unaccountably, to this book. Finally, I want to acknowledge David Diop and the diffuse but, to me, quite apparent influence of his short novel *At Night All Blood Is Black*, which I translated, on this one. Once it became visible to me, I could have tried to superficially disguise it, but decided instead to make grateful note of it here. Books beget books.

No part of this work has been published previously, but three performance opportunities were crucial to its development. Thank you to the curators and audiences at the University of Buffalo's department of English, the Lab in San Francisco, and the Poetic Research Bureau in Los Angeles. For feedback on early drafts, I'm grateful to Anitra Budd, Claire Donato, Emmalea Russo, Margaux Williamson, and the writing group of Bushel Collective. Thanks to Claire Vaye Watkins for Nothingness Flats: one day we will meet and I will thank you properly. Thanks to Robin McLean, Alan Felsenthal, and Dion Graham for taking care of me that night.

I wrote the first draft in 2020 and 2021, while in and out of states of lockdown and of recovery from an accident and subsequent surgeries, which left me reliant on others in unaccustomed ways and unable to show up for others in accustomed ways. (I also felt the combination of student-loan forgiveness and pandemic relief materially, about which there is much more to say.) I will never forget the care and comradeship of my friends and family during that time, especially Pareesa, Mina, Trevor, Marco, Juliette, Simone, Desmond, Everett, Amy, Brown, Mercedes, Mark, Emily, my parents and brother, Bushel and Ugly Duckling Presse, and the warmest and most thoughtful students and colleagues an injured, remote-teaching adjunct could wish for. So many more.

Maro, I loved being your only, and therefore favorite, niece. I miss you.

Jonathan, no paragraph can contain my gratitude or my love.

© Heather Phelps-Lipton

ANNA MOSCHOVAKIS is a novelist,
poet, and translator. She won the James
Laughlin Award for her poetry and
shared the 2021 International Booker
Prize with David Diop for his novel *At
Night All Blood Is Black*. A student of
herbalism, she is a member of the pub-
lishing collective Ugly Duckling Presse
and a cofounder of Bushel Collective.